JOE and the Hidden Horseshoe

JOE and the Hidden Horseshoe

VICTORIA EVELEIGH

Illustrated by Chris Eveleigh

Orion
Children's Books

First published in Great Britain in 2013
by Orion Children's Books
a division of the Orion Publishing Group Ltd
Orion House
5 Upper St Martin's Lane
London WC2H 9EA
An Hachette UK Company

1 3 5 7 9 10 8 6 4 2

A catalogue record for this book
is available from the British Library.

ISBN 978 1 4440 0591 2

Printed in Great Britain by
Clays Ltd, St Ives plc

www.orionbooks.co.uk

For John, who came to a book signing and reminded me that boys like horses too.

Chapter 1

Joe felt as empty as the living room. He walked around its new boundaries. Grubby, well-worn areas of carpet contrasted starkly with good-as-new bits where the furniture had stood, leaving a ghostly plan of how it had been ever since he could remember.

Mum bustled in with her vacuum cleaner. "Out of the way, darling. I've just got to clean round the edges before we go."

"Why? What's the point?"

"I want to make it nice for the Ingrams when they move in. It's called being considerate to others," Mum said. She switched on the vacuum and set to work.

He scowled and went into the hall, nearly tripping over some things which had been too precious to put in the removal lorry.

The front door was open. Traffic noise and a warm summer breeze wafted in from the sunlit street. The smells and sounds of the city were so familiar that for a moment Joe allowed himself to imagine nothing had changed. He was on his way to school, to aikido or to play football with his friends in the park. This was his life. It couldn't just vanish. Could it?

Dad hurried up the front steps, walked straight past Joe and shouted up the stairs, "Emily, I need those goldfish *now*!"

"Okay!" Emily's voice called back. "I'm just making holes in the roof."

"You're *what*?"

"Making holes in the roof of the goldfish container."

"Oh." Dad sighed. "Help me take this stuff out to the car, will you, Joe?"

The car was parked a long way down the street. "One thing I won't miss is the constant battle to find a parking space," Dad said as he marched along the hot pavement. It was the first time he'd admitted he'd miss anything. When anybody asked about it, he always said his new job as the head of a group of village primary schools was "a dream come true" and "the opportunity of a lifetime".

"What'll you miss?" Joe asked, hoping Dad was having second thoughts.

"The same sort of things as you, I expect," Dad said, giving Joe a rueful smile. "Friends and neighbours, football matches at Villa Park, Granny and Grandpa a couple of streets away ..." His words trailed off and he looked sad for a moment before smiling. "But I know this move is the right thing for us as a family. It'll be great to get away from it all, and you'll soon make new friends."

I don't want to get away from anything, Joe thought, and I don't want new friends. I'm perfectly happy with "it all" here and with the friends I've got already, thank you very much.

The things were packed away into the car, and they walked back to the house in silence.

Mum was waiting with the vacuum cleaner. "Here we are. You can put it in the car now," she said.

"There's no room, Jackie. There really isn't," Dad replied.

"There *has* to be." Mum insisted. "I'll have it on my lap if necessary."

"Okay, up to you." Dad went to the bottom of the stairs. "Do hurry up, Emily!"

Emily gradually came into view – pink sandals,

multicoloured sundress, silver-blonde hair held back with pink butterfly hairclips – walking carefully down the stairs, carrying six goldfish floating in a large plastic ice cream container.

"Right then," Dad said firmly. "Has everyone got everything?"

Joe seized the chance to put off the inevitable for a few minutes longer. "I'll just go and check."

"Well, if you must."

Joe ran upstairs to his bedroom one last time. Like the sitting room, it looked much larger now and there were marks etched onto the carpet where the furniture had been. The same feeling of emptiness overwhelmed him. The house was dead. All its insides had been ripped out. It wasn't home any longer.

He scuffed his foot against the frayed patch of carpet which Rex, his hamster, had chewed in an attempt to make a nest under the bed. Rex had lived to a good age, despite being a brilliant escapologist, but he'd died just over a year ago. Joe didn't have a pet now. He'd wanted a dog ever since he could remember, but Mum and Dad had said it was out of the question while they were living in Birmingham and working full-time as teachers.

One good thing about moving to the country was he'd been promised a dog. It looked as if they'd have horses and ponies as well, because Mum and Emily were determined to get one, or two, or as many as possible. Joe was sure Emily would hate the hard work of actually looking after one – she wouldn't even clean out her goldfish because it made her feel sick – but she was ridiculously excited about it all.

"We've got to go now!" Dad called from the hallway.

Joe said a final farewell to his bedroom, and ran downstairs.

Dad followed him through the front door, locked it, hesitated for a moment, then posted the keys through the letterbox.

That's it, Joe thought. We don't live here anymore.

Chapter 2

The car was full to bursting with people and possessions. Dad drove, anxiously checking his wing mirrors the whole time because the view out of the back window was completely blocked. Mum sat in the front passenger seat, hugging the vacuum cleaner.

Joe and Emily were unable to move for luggage. The goldfish container was wedged on the car seat between them. When the car changed direction or speed, water leaked out of the ventilation holes and dribbled onto the seat.

Nobody said a word. Dad turned on the radio. One of Joe's favourite songs came on. For a moment it lifted his mood, but then Emily started to sing along tunelessly. He glared at her.

She smiled her most annoying smile, and carried on.

He gritted his teeth and stared out of the window. The streets became less familiar, then turned into a dual carriageway, then a motorway. As their old life slipped away, their new one became unavoidable. The level of water in the fish container sank, drip by drip, until Emily convinced herself her pets would die. She started to cry. Dad pulled into a motorway service station, and they all struggled out of the car.

Joe's jeans had a large damp patch where they'd been in contact with the car seat. It looked as if Emily had a similar problem with her dress. He couldn't resist saying, "Ha! Ha! You've wet yourself!"

She lunged towards him, arms outstretched, ready to push.

Instinctively, he pivoted to the right.

She fell onto the rough tarmac of the car park, saving herself with her right hand. There was a pause while she lifted her hand up and inspected it. Blood oozed out of her grazed palm. She sobbed hysterically.

"Joe! Now look what you've done!" Mum shouted, helping Emily to her feet and hugging her close.

"I didn't even touch her!" Joe said.

Mum stroked Emily's silky blonde hair. "You must have, or she wouldn't have fallen over like that."

Joe wanted to explain that by swerving he'd used Emily's attacking energy against her, causing her to overbalance and fall flat on her face. It was a classic aikido move. He was sorry that Emily had hurt herself, and he'd been just about to say so. The moment had been taken away, though.

"At the very least you could apologise, rather than just standing there scowling," Mum said.

Dad managed to find some jumpers in the car for Joe and Emily to tie round their waists so nobody would see their wet bottoms. Then they went to find bottles of cold mineral water for the fish container and a first aid kit, loos and refreshments for themselves.

It was the second week of the summer holidays. The service station was heaving with families, and there was a buzz of excitement about the place. Toys, travel pillows and sun tan lotion were being whisked through the checkout along with food, drink and newspapers. Joe looked on enviously as a mother gave her son money for a magazine and some sweets. He wished his family were going away for a week or two, safe in the knowledge they'd be coming home again. Instead, they were temporarily homeless, mid-way between one life and another. If there was a feeling opposite to a holiday feeling, this was it.

"Are we nearly there yet?" Emily asked for the millionth time.

To Joe's surprise Dad said, "Yes, nearly there."

They drove past some cottages, down a hill, over a bridge, up a hill and turned right at a crossroads. It was then that Joe recognised where they were. They'd visited three months ago, but spring had turned into summer and everything seemed different. The lane was narrow, with a wide grassy verge followed by a fence. A golden crop of something shimmered in the field beyond. The early evening sunshine cast long shadows everywhere.

An elegant dark brown horse with an arched neck trotted by on the grass verge. The young man riding it smiled, raised his hand and called, "Thank you," as Dad slowed the car to a crawl.

"Oooh! Look!" Emily cried, waving frantically and jumping up and down on the car seat, causing mini tsunamis in the fish container.

Mum bent herself round the vacuum cleaner, straining to get a better view. "Lovely!" she whispered.

Joe hoped the rider couldn't see through the car's tinted windows. Mum and Emily were so embarrassing; as soon as they saw anything from a seaside donkey to a police horse they went completely stupid.

Mum had tried to instil a similar love of horses in Joe by enrolling him in the Saturday kids' club at a riding stables on the outskirts of Birmingham. She'd almost succeeded, as he'd really enjoyed being around horses. He hadn't enjoyed being the only boy in his group, though, nor trotting in endless circles around a dusty indoor school. The ponies all seemed to have perfected the art of using just enough energy to get by, but only when pushed, so riding was always an effort, like pedalling a bike uphill. The poor things must have been bored senseless doing the same exercises day in, day out, with an assortment of children kicking their sides and pulling on their mouths. Joe had longed to go out for a proper ride – galloping, jumping and having fun – but they'd never been allowed to leave the confines of the school.

Eventually football had started to compete for Joe's Saturdays, and when Emily had started riding it had been the final straw. Even at the age of six, she'd known how to show him up at every opportunity.

Joe hadn't ridden for several years now, but the horse trotting past him made him think. If he had a beautiful animal like that and masses of countryside to gallop over, he wouldn't mind taking up riding again – he wouldn't mind it at all.

Emily shouted, "Look, here's the bridge!"

The bridge was made out of concrete and metal, and the car made a peculiar rumbling noise as they drove over it.

Shortly afterwards, they turned left through an open gate, bumped along a short driveway and came to a halt behind two removal lorries. Their furniture and belongings were already being unloaded onto a mossy area in front of the house, adding to the untidy look of the place. Plants of various shapes and sizes, presumably weeds, grew randomly here and there. Joe was sure it hadn't been like that when they'd visited it in April. The whole place looked unloved and unwelcoming.

"Newbridge Farm. We've arrived!" Dad said.

Chapter 3

It soon became clear that the people who'd sold Newbridge Farm hadn't shared Mum's concern about making life easy for its new owners. Everything which could be removed had been taken away, including light bulbs, lamp shades, curtains and carpets. The floorboards were littered with dusty debris and old carpet tacks.

"I was right to bring my vacuum cleaner," Mum said as she hurried upstairs to clear away the worst of the mess before the furniture was unloaded.

Emily and Joe followed her up the creaking

staircase, anxious to lay claim to their rooms even though that had all been decided in April.

There was a narrow landing near the top. To the left several stairs led to a long corridor, and to the right there was a lone room. In a bid for independence, Joe had chosen it as his bedroom. He wasn't so sure now, but he didn't want to say anything.

The door scraped against the floor as he opened it. Swirling dust and a musty smell greeted him. Joe remembered his old bedroom with its deep carpet, straight walls, high ceiling, central heating and large double-glazed window. How on earth could he even begin to make this dingy cell his own? Where would he put all his stuff, for starters? Despair seeped into him like a sponge taking up water.

He went downstairs and outside to the car, weaving between stacks of furniture and piles of boxes. He prised his laptop from the boot of the car, and took it back to his room. In his absence, the removal men had somehow managed to get his bed in there. It looked out of place in its new surroundings but, even with a bare mattress, it felt comfortingly familiar when he sat down and switched on the computer. As he waited for it to load, his chair, bookcase and bedside table were also delivered, together with several boxes of belongings.

His old bedroom had been fitted with drawers, a

wardrobe and a desk, but there was nothing built into this room, unless you counted an old fireplace in the far wall.

A message appeared on his laptop screen: the usual internet connection couldn't be detected. *Search for a new connection?*

Joe clicked *Yes*.

More boxes and a large plastic bag full of posters were delivered while Joe waited. His computer seemed to be on a go-slow. He sat looking at the screen, not wanting to acknowledge a growing sense of apprehension. It usually didn't take this long … Eventually another message popped up: *connection not available*.

Joe stared at the message in disbelief. The internet was his lifeline, his vital link to friends and the outside world. How could it vanish when he needed it so much? He heard Dad's voice downstairs.

"Dad! The internet's not working!" he shouted, still sitting on the bed.

"I can't hear you!" Dad called up the stairs. "Come down."

Joe was reluctant to take his eyes off the computer, in case it miraculously worked all of a sudden, but he went downstairs and repeated, "The internet's not working."

"Yes, I know," Dad said. "I'm afraid you'll have to

cope without it for a while. There's no telephone or internet connection at the moment. It's on our 'to do' list, don't worry."

"*Don't worry!*" Joe echoed in disbelief. "How am I supposed to survive if there's no internet? It's a disaster!"

"I think a sense of proportion's needed here," Dad said in his composed schoolteacher voice which meant he was annoyed and choosing his words carefully. "'Disaster' is usually a term reserved for earthquakes, floods, famines and other life-threatening situations, not a temporary inability to access the internet. Right now I'm more concerned about finding the microwave because there's no oil in the tank, which means the oil-fired cooker won't work. Oh, and there'll be no hot water either, I'm afraid."

Emily came clattering downstairs. "Dad, where's the telly? It's nearly time for *Fame and Fortune.*"

"Sorry, Pumpkin. The TV won't work for a few days. We can't get a satellite dish fixed up until next week."

"Can I watch *Fame and Fortune* on your laptop, Joe?" Emily wheedled.

"No. There's no internet connection either," Joe said.

"But there's nothing to do!" Emily wailed.

"Don't be silly. There are a hundred and one things you can do. Unpack some of your belongings, for a start," Dad said.

"Can't. There's nowhere to put anything," Emily said.

"Okay, then. Why don't you read a book?" Dad suggested.

"Bor-ring," Emily sang.

Dad looked heavenwards. "I despair sometimes. What do you think people did before televisions and computers were invented?"

"Rode dinosaurs?" Emily asked.

Dad laughed.

Joe took his phone out of his pocket and searched for new messages, turning his face away so Emily couldn't see he was smiling at her remark. No phone signal either. What's wrong with this place? It's stuck in the Dark Ages, he thought. "I'm off outside," he mumbled.

"I want to come too," Emily said.

He sighed. "I'm not going to do anything exciting."

"Don't mind."

Joe didn't know much about phones, but he reckoned he'd have more chance of picking up a signal on higher ground, so he went to the entrance and started walking up the road. Emily followed him, pretending to canter like a pony. He concentrated on his signal icon, and tried his best to ignore her.

A signal, at last! He checked his phone for messages. There weren't any. Where were his friends when he needed them? Enjoying the summer holidays, no doubt. Perhaps they'd been trying to contact him via the internet. He sent some texts to tell them his computer wasn't working.

"That's a funny house," Emily said.

Joe looked up from his phone and saw a small bungalow, not much bigger than a mobile home, surrounded by a wooden fence. Smoke drifted from a metal chimney on the corrugated iron roof. A couple of brightly coloured blankets hung on a washing line, and chickens scratched around in the garden. A tortoiseshell cat sat on the doorstep, licking its paws. The door was dark green, decorated with gold and red swirls, and there was a large horseshoe nailed above it. The green window frames had the same elaborate paintwork.

A woman's face appeared at the window, looking straight at them, so they fled.

Soon Emily reverted to being a pony again. This time, apparently, she was a nervous pony called Frisky, shying and snorting at the shadows which stretched like tentacles over the ground.

Give me strength, Joe thought.

At that moment there was the sound of hooves on

tarmac. Looking round, Joe saw a girl on a dark brown pony trotting down the road. The pony bowled along eagerly, head high and ears pricked.

Emily hurried towards them.

"Hi, lovely evening," the girl said as she drew near. She wore a light blue polo shirt with the number seven on it, faded denim jeans and short riding boots. Brown shoulder-length hair escaped from under her riding hat, and her bare arms were suntanned.

Emily's voice was squeaky with excitement. "Hi, I love your pony. What's it called?"

The girl grinned. She had incredibly white teeth. "He's called Treacle." She stroked her pony's shoulder, which shone like polished wood in the evening sunshine. "Are you here on holiday?"

"No, we've just moved into the house down there," Emily said, pointing. "My name's Emily, and this is my brother, Joe."

The girl gave Joe a brief half-smile before turning back to Emily. "We're practically next door neighbours, then. My dad owns Lucketts Farm." She pointed back up the hill. "Do you ride?"

"Oh, yes!" Emily said. "I love horses!"

Joe wanted to say that he actually liked horses too, and could ride much better than Emily, but he couldn't get a word in edgeways. The girls chatted non-stop, bonding instantly through ponies despite the fact Emily was several years younger. He learned the girl was called Caroline Cox, and her father was a farmer who owned point-to-point racehorses. She had a three-year-old younger brother called Angus, plus a step-brother who was grown up. Treacle was 12.1 hands high and was a registered Dartmoor pony with the absurd name of Kingstonhaugh Short But Sweet. Caroline said she wasn't into showing, so she never had to use his registered name, thank goodness. Treacle loved hacking and Pony Club games, but he wasn't so keen on dressage and show jumping. That was okay because Caroline liked gymkhana games best of all. Her Dad wanted her to get a bigger, better pony but she'd "rather die than sell Treacle", she said. One of their thoroughbred horses had just had an adorable foal, Pony Club camp was starting on Monday ... The excited babble about horses and ponies went on and on.

Joe felt as if he'd become invisible. The girls at the riding stables had been the same, jealously guarding their exclusive right to horse-talk. Who'd made the rule that only girls should be keen on riding? Had it always been like that? How could men become jockeys, show jumpers, eventers, mounted policemen or anything to do with horses if boys didn't ride?

Treacle cropped the long grass, his bit clanking gently as he munched his way methodically along the verge. Joe longed to get closer, to stroke Treacle and breathe in that lovely horse smell, but he just stood there, looking. I wonder if Caroline realises how lucky she is, he thought.

"Well, I'd better go before Treacle gorges himself," Caroline said. "He has to be on a strict diet in the summer, poor thing, so this grass must be like a pile of sweets."

"Yes, we'd better be going too," Joe said.

Caroline glanced at him in surprise, as if she'd completely forgotten he was there. "Bye, then. Come and see our foal sometime." She gathered up her reins and set Treacle off at a canter.

Joe stared at the pony and rider with a twinge of envy, not sure whether he'd been invited to see the foal or not and trying to tell himself he didn't care anyway.

"Bye, Caroline! See you soon!" Emily shouted. Then she set off at an imaginary canter after them, down the road to Newbridge Farm.

Joe hoped Caroline wouldn't look back and see her. Emily's by far the most embarrassing girl I've ever met, he thought. Just my luck she's my sister.

Chapter 4

The following week was so boring that Joe found it hard to get up in the morning. It was easier to lie in bed and stare at the crazy pattern of cracks and damp patches on the ceiling than to "do something useful", especially as he wasn't sleeping at all well.

Before, he'd always gone to sleep without giving it a second thought, oblivious to the familiar city noises. But this place gave him the creeps. It didn't help that there were no street lights, so his room was pitch black at night. He woke at the slightest noise: scampering creatures in the attic, creaking floorboards, wind moaning in the chimney or an owl calling *"Whooo! Whu-whoo!"* from the tree outside his bedroom window. So much for the peace and quiet of the countryside.

It was hard to tell which was worse, the nights or the days. Anything which counted as "doing something useful" was hard work, or boring, or both: unpacking, moving furniture, cleaning and decorating the house, clearing away rubbish or attempting to dig an area which Mum had decided would be her vegetable garden. The fact that Joe found digging the concrete-hard soil the most enjoyable job, or the least unenjoyable, spoke volumes about the alternatives. At least it was outside.

The man who'd ridden past the car as they were arriving seemed to use the road a lot for exercising a succession of beautiful horses. Joe always waved as he clattered by, and the man raised a hand and smiled in return.

There was no sign of Caroline and Treacle. Joe supposed they were at Pony Club camp.

Apart from Caroline, he'd only come across one other person his age, and that was Martin, the son of the people who owned the Ewe and Lamb pub. Joe had met him when they'd gone to Coltridge, their nearest village, for a pub supper. Martin had immediately latched onto Joe, asking if he'd like to go fishing. When he'd said he didn't think he'd enjoy fishing, Martin had suggested a trip into town to see a film or something instead.

Joe hadn't needed to *make* friends before. He'd known most of his good mates in Birmingham since pre-school. Their parents all knew each other and their friendships had grown naturally. Now he realised how much he'd taken his friends for granted. It had been almost impossible to stay in touch properly since he'd moved to Newbridge Farm. There was still no internet, so contact had been limited to a few texts and some rushed telephone conversations while Joe was standing near the painted bungalow to pick up a signal. His best mates were especially difficult to get hold of. Rahul was on holiday with his family in Cornwall and John always seemed to be out visiting people, going swimming, playing football or practising aikido. All the things Joe would be doing, if only ...

Mum had said they'd have much more freedom in the countryside, but Joe felt like a prisoner. In Birmingham he'd been able to move around by himself, walking and using buses to go and see his friends and do things. Here he was totally dependent on his parents for transport, unless he walked four miles into Coltridge to catch a bus. There were three buses into town each day from Monday to Friday, two on Saturday and none on Sunday – hardly worth the bother.

Could time really go at different speeds? Did clocks run more slowly in the countryside? Every hour of every day seemed to drag, whereas in Birmingham the hours had sped by, especially in the holidays. Granny always said "time flies when you're enjoying yourself". Well, the opposite's also true, Joe thought: time drags when you're not.

By the end of the week he was well and truly fed up. He went on strike, refusing to do any more work. "It's supposed to be the holidays," he said. "We should be having fun."

"Well, go and have some fun, then," Mum said in an exasperated voice. "There's plenty of lovely countryside out there, waiting to be explored, and all you can do is sit around moaning."

This struck Joe as particularly unfair, considering the hours he'd spent digging, but he just said, "Fine, I'm off."

"Wait for me," said Emily.

Joe groaned, but was secretly glad of an ally.

They made for the bridge, and spent a happy half hour playing Pooh sticks until a lorry nearly knocked into Emily as she ran across the road to watch her stick appear. Rattled, they moved on, looking for something else to do. The large fields on each side had crops growing in neat rows and, although they hadn't a clue what the crops were, they knew it would be wrong to trample over them. A car sped by, forcing them to jump onto the verge.

"It's much more dangerous going for a walk here than it was in Birmingham," Joe said.

Emily turned round. "I want to go back."

"No, let's at least get to the top of the hill," Joe replied. He couldn't admit defeat by returning so soon.

As they walked, he remembered a television programme about a blind woman who'd moved to the country. She'd been talking about how lost she'd felt, even though she had a guide dog, because in the countryside there were no pavements and hardly any points of reference or people to ask for directions. Joe could imagine what she'd felt like. Even with good eyesight, he found it hard to know where to go or what to do when he got there.

They carried on walking. Now there was a green field on the right. It looked as if it had grass growing in it, although it was hard to tell because it had been cut short like a huge, rough lawn. There was a gate with a wooden signpost.

"A bridlepath," Joe said. "Let's see where it leads. At least it'll be off the road."

"Do we *have* to? I want to go *home*," Emily whined.

"Well, this is in the right direction," he said, trying to be upbeat. He still couldn't bring himself to call Newbridge Farm "home". It felt as if it was the setting for an experimental lifestyle programme which had gone horribly wrong – one of those TV documentaries where families had to live in an old hovel like their forefathers and suffer unimaginable hardships, like no internet.

They went through the gate and followed a broad track of hoof prints over the field. Emily cheered up when she saw them, but unfortunately it inspired her to behave like a pony yet again. She ran along with splayed out legs, trying to place each foot in the imprint of a horseshoe.

It looks as if she's wearing a wet nappy, Joe thought, but with immense self-control he stopped himself from saying so. Luckily there was no one else to witness Emily's ridiculous behaviour.

In the far corner of the field there was a huge stack of big round things covered in black plastic.

"What are they?" Emily asked.

"Silage bales," Joe said. He'd learned about them in geography. "They're giant rolls of grass wrapped in plastic." He prodded a bale. It felt warm and squidgy in the midday sun. The wrapping was like thick cling film wound round and round each bale.

"Let's climb to the top," she suggested, and she started to scramble up the side of the nearest one.

Joe chose a place further along the stack and climbed as fast as he could, anxious to prove he was the fittest. His fingers clung to the bales and his trainers tore at the plastic.

The view from the top was incredible. Joe studied it in detail, getting his bearings, reading the landscape like a map. Beneath him the river meandered gently along its valley. He could see a small bridge below, and guessed the bridlepath crossed there before climbing up the other side of the valley to a great mass of grey barns and silos which he reckoned was Lucketts Farm. It looked rather like an industrial estate, especially compared to Newbridge Farm. From a distance, Joe had to admit, their little farm was as pretty as a storybook picture, with its compact house and farmyard: stables and sheds on one side and a large old-fashioned barn on the other. The orchard and fields – five in all – were separated by plump dark green hedges, whereas the fields beyond were huge and their hedges were sparse or non-existent ...

"What on *earth* do you think you're doing?" An angry voice shouted.

Joe nearly jumped out of his skin. He looked down, and saw a tall man mounted on a large grey horse. A black Labrador dog stood by his side, panting and waving its tail uncertainly, and a girl on a dark brown pony was behind them.

Caroline and Treacle. They must be back from Pony Club camp, Joe thought. Hoping for a bit of moral support, he searched for Emily, but she was nowhere to be seen. He had to say something in reply. "Sorry, I was just looking at the scenery."

"*Looking at the scenery*!" The man echoed his words, emphasising their stupidity. He came closer to the base of the stack. "My farm isn't a ruddy playground, you know. I don't doubt there's a fine view from up there, but from here I can only see damaged bales which will need to be patched up immediately so our silage isn't ruined." He stopped talking, and turned to hear something Caroline was saying. "My daughter tells me you've just moved into Newbridge Farm and you're called Joe."

She's remembered my name, Joe thought fleetingly.

"I'm sorry our first meeting hasn't been more cordial, Joe," the man continued, "and I hope we'll all get along fine once you've learned how to behave in the countryside. Now, please get down *carefully* and go home."

Joe slid down the squeaky plastic as carefully as he could, and landed in an undignified heap. Now he knew what people meant when they talked about dying of embarrassment. "Sorry," he mumbled, and walked back across the field self-consciously.

Ambling down the road to the bridge, he saw a creature on the grassy verge. It looked like a frog, but it was larger, with a dry, warty skin. It must be a toad, he thought, and bent down to pick it up for a closer look. At that moment he heard the quick thud of footsteps, and saw Emily running to catch him up. She was grinning. Unbelievable.

"That was so *funny*!" she gasped. "You should have hidden behind the bales with me. Didn't you see the farmer coming?"

"No," Joe said acidly. "Why didn't you *tell* me, you little creep?"

"Wasn't time. When you slid down that plastic it sounded as if you were farting!" Emily said, and burst into helpless giggles.

In one quick movement, Joe put the toad on Emily's head.

She let out an ear-splitting scream and shook her head violently. The toad flopped into the grass by the side of the road and shuffled away, but Emily kept on screaming and clawing at her hair for a while. Then, wild-eyed, she ran for home.

*

As usual, she got the last laugh. When Joe arrived home, Mum was waiting for him, ready with a long lecture about how disappointed she was that he couldn't be trusted to take care of his little sister.

He wanted to shout, "Can't you see? She's so *annoying*! Why do you always blame me?" but he'd learned that it was easier to switch off, say nothing and wait for the storm to pass.

Afterwards, he ran upstairs, dived onto his bed and lay with his face buried in a pillow. "I *hate* this place! I hate, hate, hate it! Nothing's gone right since we moved here. *I want to go home!*"

Chapter 5

J oe avoided lunch, insisting he wasn't hungry, and went outside to make further inroads into Mum's would-be vegetable garden. He needed to get rid of his pent-up anger somehow. Again and again he slammed his spade into the hard soil. Each time, a jolt ran up his arms and down through his body, shaking up his thoughts until they didn't seem to matter or make sense any more.

Clink!

He lifted the spade up and tried again.

Clink!

Metal on stone made a *clunk* noise, but this was different. It sounded more like metal hitting metal. He knelt down to inspect the soil. A wide, curved, rusty thing with spikes sticking out of it was embedded in the wall of the trench he'd been digging. Perhaps it was an ancient piece of jewellery or something. He tried to pull it out, but it wouldn't move.

Getting up again, he caught sight of a woman looking over the fence. She was short and broad, with a round, weather-beaten face and grey-black hair. The tortoiseshell cat he'd seen outside the brightly painted bungalow came into the field for a moment and then darted back to the woman. She must be the owner of the bungalow, he thought.

"Afternoon," she said.

"Hi," Joe replied.

"Found something?"

"Think so." Joe picked up his spade and dug into the soil around where he thought the rest of the object might be. Eventually he managed to prise it out. It looked like an old horseshoe, swollen with rust, complete with bent nails in the holes. What a disappointment.

He took it over to show the woman standing by the fence, and was surprised when she said solemnly, "You are blessed. A lucky horseshoe."

The woman introduced herself as Nellie Reeve. As Joe had guessed, she lived in Orchard Rise, the bungalow just up the hill. He introduced himself, but she already knew his name.

Nellie told Joe that his horseshoe was especially lucky because it had seven nail holes and had been found with the nails intact, pointing upwards. It was a big shoe, so it had probably come off a carthorse. Quite old, as well – at least a hundred years, most likely. She said it would make an ideal wishing shoe.

"What's a wishing shoe?" Joe asked. "Is it like the horseshoe you've got above your door?"

"No, that's Molly's shoe. It protects my house."

"Who's Molly?"

"The best mare I ever had. Took us to Appleby Fair every year, towing our vardo all the way there and back again."

"What's a vardo?"

"A living wagon. Gypsy caravans, some people call them."

"Are you a gypsy?" Joe couldn't believe it. She didn't look much like a gypsy, with her short-sleeved shirt, navy blue trousers and lace-up shoes.

"I prefer to be called a Romany."

A real live gypsy, I mean Romany, Joe thought.

How cool is that? He stared at the lumpy crescent of metal in his hand. "Do I just hold this and make a wish, then?"

"Depends," Nellie replied. "How many wishes do you want?"

"As many as possible, I suppose."

"Well, you've got seven holes there, so there's seven wishes if you have a mind to turn it into a proper wishing shoe."

"Yes, okay," Joe said uncertainly. "How do I do that?"

"First you'll have to brush the rust off and remove the nails so the holes are open. Then, when it gets dark, you should light a red candle in a room with no other source of light. Sit in front of the candle and write seven wishes on seven coloured pieces of paper. The colour depends on the wish, but I can write them all down for you if you like because there are quite a few to remember. After you've finished, hide the horseshoe in a box and put it somewhere safe."

I bet she's having me on. She'll be bringing out her crystal ball and trying to sell me lucky heather next, Joe thought.

As if reading his mind, Nellie said, "Don't do this if you don't believe in it, though. Your wishes will only come true if you put your heart and soul into them, and they should always be made with love."

Her dark brown eyes looked earnestly at him. "Your thoughts and words are much more powerful than you realise, so be careful what you wish for." She bent down and stroked the cat, which was sitting looking at her expectantly. "Goodbye, Joe. Drop in sometime if you're passing. *Kushti bok* – good luck."

"Kushti bok," Joe repeated. It sounded like a password into a secret world. "Kushti bok – good luck." He turned, and saw his mum coming out of the back door, carrying a tray. Quickly, he dropped the horseshoe into the trench he'd dug and covered it with earth.

As Mum came closer, Joe saw there was a glass of orange squash, a sandwich, an apple and some chocolate on the tray she was carrying.

"Peace offering," she said, holding it out and giving Joe a tight-lipped "I'm sorry" smile.

"Thanks," Joe said, taking the drink in one hand and the sandwich in the other. Cheese and pickle – his favourite. He was starving.

"I do realise how boring it's been for you this past week, darling," Mum said. "But Dad and I have got so much to do at the moment. I know it hasn't been easy for you, but we're all in this together and it'll be worth it, I promise. If we can just get the main things sorted, we'll be able to get some normality back into our lives. In fact, once I've got the spare room fixed you could have one or two friends to stay. You'd like that, wouldn't you?"

"Mm," Joe mumbled through a mouthful of cheese and pickle. In theory it would be great to have a friend to stay, but what would they do all day? Dig holes?

"Oh, and talking of friends," Mum added, "last night Dad was talking to Nigel, the landlord in the Ewe and Lamb, and it turns out that his son Martin does aikido! Isn't that amazing? *Anyway*, apparently there's a training place— "

"Dojo," Joe corrected her.

"Yes, a *dojo* in town, in Bellsham, and Martin goes every Saturday afternoon. He's a blue belt, like you. The place is closed for a couple of weeks so the teacher can have a holiday, but Nigel's very kindly offered to give you a lift there when lessons start again. That'll be something to look forward to, won't it?

"Yup," he said, unable to summon the enthusiasm she seemed to be expecting, and stuffed the rest of the sandwich into his mouth so he wouldn't be able to say any more.

When Mum had gone, he unearthed the old horseshoe, carried it back to the house and managed to take it up to his room without anyone seeing.

He sat on his bed with the arc of rusty metal balanced in his hands, and tried to imagine what the horse who'd worn the shoe had looked like. Had it been slow and steady or excitable and difficult to control? Maybe it had lost the shoe while it had been ploughing the same ground he'd been digging? The image of two big, strong Shire horses standing shoulder to shoulder came from nowhere and lodged in his mind. Yes, they'd been ploughing – he was sure of that now – and the shoe had been ploughed into the ground and lost forever. Well, not quite forever.

Perhaps he should make it into a wishing shoe. Joe turned it over, trying to gauge how difficult it would be to remove the nails. He certainly needed some good luck at the moment, but how could this old, misshapen lump of junk help? If horseshoes really were lucky, surely everyone would carry them around and nobody would have bad luck. No, it was just superstitious nonsense. And yet – it was daft, of course, but he couldn't help wondering . . .

"Joe? Are you up there? I'm going into town for some paint. Do you want to come?" Dad called up the stairs.

"Yup, coming!" Joe shouted. He tucked the horseshoe under some clothes in a large cardboard box, and hurried downstairs.

Chapter 6

O n Sunday, Mum and Emily went out all day together. They came back bursting with the news that they'd bought two ponies called Lady and Lightning.

"Buy one, get one free," Mum said cheerfully.

"That's all very well when you're buying loo rolls or cereal, Jackie, but not *ponies*!" Dad protested. "If they're being given away like that there must be something wrong with them."

Mum looked sheepish. "Not really. Lady was pretty expensive, actually, but Mrs Peters, the owner, said if we bought Lady she'd let us have Lightning for free because they're best friends and Lightning's slightly unsound."

"Unsound! What does that mean? Not right in the head?"

"No, she's just a bit lame, that's all, but she's got a sweet nature and she'll be a good companion. Emily can ride her on a leading rein until we find the right pony for her. You loved Lightning, didn't you, darling?" Mum said, beaming at Emily.

Emily ran to Dad and hugged him. "I love, love, love her!" she cried, giving him lots of little kisses. Then she pranced around the kitchen table.

Mummy's pet, Joe thought darkly.

Dad sighed. "I thought you were just going to take a look! You promised you'd ask for a second opinion before you got anything. You should have shopped around a bit, not bought the first thing you saw."

"Yes, I know, but Mrs Peters said there was someone else interested and they were going to try Lady out this evening, so if I wanted her I should say so there and then. I couldn't let her go. She's perfect!"

A perfect pony called Lady sounds sort of promising, Joe thought. Perhaps I could ride her too.

"I've got some pictures of her," Mum said eagerly. She rummaged around in her handbag, pulled out

39

her phone and switched it on. "There, isn't she gorgeous?" She passed it to Dad.

He frowned. "Looks more like a black-and-white cow to me."

"Brian! Don't be so horrid," Mum replied, taking her phone back. "There's an old horsey saying, you know: a good horse is never a bad colour."

Emily stopped for a moment. "What does that mean?" she asked.

"It means that the colour of a horse shouldn't make any difference when you're deciding whether you like it or not," Mum answered.

"Like with people?"

"Yes, like with people," Mum said, smiling.

"Can I have a look?" Joe asked.

Mum handed him the phone.

What a disappointment. The pony didn't look like a Lady at all. She had a big head, long body and thick, hairy legs which were much shorter than they should have been for the size of the rest of her. And it was hard to ignore her random black and white splodges. It was if a toddler had been told to colour her in and had lost interest half way through. She definitely wasn't the sort of horse he'd hoped Mum would get. "What's the other one like?" he asked.

"I took a few of her as well – she's there somewhere," Mum replied.

He flicked through the photos. There were certainly plenty of the black-and-white creature, and it didn't look good from any angle ... "Wow!" A striking-looking pony with a wide white blaze and large, intelligent eyes looked straight at him. "Is it the chestnut one?"

"Yes. She's stunning, isn't she? And she's got beautiful manners. You enjoyed riding her, didn't you, Pumpkin?"

Emily nodded enthusiastically.

"So you did at least try them out?" Dad queried.

"Honestly, Brian, I'm not stupid, you know! We went for a lovely ride over some fields. I rode Lady, and Mrs Peters rode her horse and led Emily on Lightning. They only walked, of course, but I even had a little canter. It was so thrilling – took me right back to my childhood. I knew there and then that Lady was meant for me. She's only 14.3 hands high, so she's technically a pony, but she feels like a horse when you're on her. Ideal, as I really don't need anything too big. It would have been foolish to buy a thoroughbred as a first horse, wouldn't it?"

No, Joe thought. A thoroughbred would have been ideal. I'd have ridden a thoroughbred.

"Much better to have a safe, solid, dependable type. *A bombproof hack*, that's what Mrs Peters said she is," Mum continued. A dreamy look came over her. "Lady and Lightning – it has a nice ring to it, doesn't it?"

Dad looked exasperated. "So you asked lots of questions about their history and why they were for sale, did you?"

"*Do* stop interrogating me like this! I've told you already, we spent ages there. Mrs Peters couldn't have been nicer. She's not a crooked dealer or anything, if that's what you're thinking. She wants to deliver them herself, and she's even sold us their tack, so that proves it's a genuine sale, doesn't it?"

"Why? I don't see that proves anything."

Mum sighed. "If she didn't care about them, she wouldn't have offered to deliver them, would she? And private owners have tack for a specific pony, so it's of no use if the pony's gone – see?"

Dad's expression showed he wasn't convinced.

"If you must know, they're only being sold because her daughter's going to university," Mum added before he could say anything.

"Mm, it seems an odd mixture of equines for a girl of that age to own."

"Brian, why do you have to be so *suspicious* of everyone? This is a dream come true for me, you know. I've always wanted my own horse and, now that it's happening at long last, all you can do is pour cold water on the whole thing." Mum's voice quavered.

"Okay, okay," Dad said. "Go ahead and get them, but on your head be it."

"What does that mean?" Emily asked.

"Don't blame me if things go wrong," Dad replied.

"Nothing's going to go wrong, is it, Mummy?"

"No, of course not, darling," Mum said with a bright smile.

Chapter 7

J oe had never seen his mum so excited about anything. She pressed the family into action, tidying the old stables, cleaning out the water troughs and checking the fields for poisonous plants and anything else which could be dangerous to horses.

After two days of hard work, they all drove to a huge warehouse which had LANDSDOWN FARMERS in big letters over the entrance.

It was like a massive supermarket for people living in the countryside, and it sold everything:

tractors and farm machinery, timber and wire, farm chemicals, fertilisers, veterinary medicines, animal feed, seed, tools, nails, screws, torches, country clothing and, of course, a huge range of items for horses and riders. Joe had never realised such places existed.

"No wonder farmers are always pleading poverty if there are stores like this all over the country," Dad said. "I can see a hundred and one things I could do with already."

Joe looked wistfully at the aisle devoted to dogs, and imagined his dream pet – a tri-coloured border collie – lying in one of the dog beds, eating food from a shiny steel bowl or playing with the vast array of doggy toys on offer.

Mum and Emily made a bee-line for the equine department. Like contestants in a supermarket dash, they filled two trolleys until they could hold no more: rugs, a couple of head collars with lead ropes, buckets, grooming kits, hay nets, fly repellent, horse shampoo ... their purchases seemed endless – and mostly pink or purple, thanks to Emily.

"There must be several pony-mad Emilys around if pink water buckets are the in-thing," Dad commented as he packed the shopping into the car. "I hope that's it now."

"Nearly," Mum said cheerfully. "I'll need feed and

bedding as well. Oh, and there'll be shoeing, of course."

Dad groaned, and shut the boot with difficulty.

Lady and Lightning were due to arrive the following afternoon. Mum's excitement was infectious, and by the time the horse trailer finally trundled into the yard Joe felt pretty keyed up too. Emily insisted on wearing her jodhpurs, riding boots and hard hat for the occasion. Joe thought she looked silly, all dressed up with no horse to ride.

At last, after several false alarms when they thought they heard a car and trailer crossing the bridge but nothing arrived, there was a distant rumble followed by the sound of a vehicle slowing down ready to turn off the road. A moment later, a smart four-wheel-drive vehicle pulling a double horsebox came into view, rattling over the potholes in the drive.

"They're here! They're here!" squealed Emily, jumping up and down.

Mrs Peters backed the trailer into the stable yard and stepped out of her truck, all smiles.

Mum let down the ramp of the trailer.

"Hang on. We'd better take Lady out first. She'll panic if she's left behind," Mrs Peters said, squeezing through the side door.

Mum looked anxious. "Does she often panic?"

"Only when she thinks her friend's leaving without her," Mrs Peters said merrily.

"Oh, so does that mean she doesn't like travelling alone?"

"I don't know, to be honest. I've never tried."

Joe knew Mum hated people saying "to be honest". She said it sounded as if being honest was unusual.

Lady's broad black-and-white bottom emerged from the back of the trailer. She trod clumsily, nearly falling off the ramp a couple of times before eventually arriving on solid ground.

Mrs Peters handed the lead rope to Joe, and disappeared again to get the other pony.

Lady's body quivered with tension as she barged around, goggle-eyed.

"Don't stand so near to her backside, Emily, she could kick you," Joe said as Emily kept trying to get close and pat her wherever her hand could reach.

Emily made a face at him, and didn't move.

Lady lifted her tail and deposited an avalanche of liquid dung onto the ground by Emily's feet, splashing her shiny boots.

"Yeeuk!" Emily exclaimed, leaping away. "Pooo-eee!"

Perfect timing. Joe tried his best not to laugh.

Lightning backed straight out of the trailer with short, careful steps. She looked around with interest, apparently accepting she was now in a new place and she'd have to make the best of it. She was larger than Joe had imagined from the photos, about 13.2 hands high at a guess. Much too big for Emily, he thought, as she dashed up to hold the lead rope with Mum.

Lady was more relaxed now she had Lightning for company. The air was filled with a sweaty horse smell mixed with something stronger and more rancid. Lady had trodden in her slithery dung several times, spreading it around so it was almost impossible to avoid. Flies were beginning to home in.

The person who named you Lady certainly had a sense of humour, Joe thought.

Mrs Peters helped Dad take the saddles and bridles to the tack room. Then she returned to her vehicle and handed him two thin books together with a neatly folded sheet of paper. "Passports and receipt for payment," she said, her tone switching in an instant from jolly to business-like. "Many thanks. Bye, then." Without so much as a glance at the ponies, she checked all the catches on the trailer, got into the car and drove away.

"What a strange woman," Dad remarked.

"I expect she was upset about leaving her ponies," Mum said.

"Mm, I doubt it, somehow. She couldn't get away fast enough. What'll we do? Put them straight into the field?"

"Well, there could be a lot of flies out there, but it'll be good for them to stretch their legs, won't it? As long as they don't gallop around and injure themselves. What do you think – stable or field?"

"I haven't a clue, Jackie. You're the expert, you decide," Dad said.

The trouble is Mum isn't an expert, Joe realised. In fact, she doesn't know much practical stuff about horses at all. The largest pet we had in Birmingham was a hamster, but now we've got two real live ponies to look after and we can't even decide where to put them! "They'll be pretty miserable in the stables, won't they? I mean, there's no hay or bedding in there yet, is there?" he said.

"I'm glad one member of our family's still capable of rational thought," Dad said. "The field it is."

Mum led the way with Lightning. Emily ran up beside her, and insisted on holding the end of the rope so she'd be leading her pony.

Joe followed with Lady, and Dad brought up the rear. Lady kept lunging forwards with her head bent round, trying to see where Dad was.

"I think she's worried about you behind her," Joe said.

"Nonsense," Dad replied. "She's supposed to be bombproof."

If you'll believe that, you'll believe anything, Joe thought, realising he may have stumbled on the truth: Mum had been so eager to get herself a horse, she'd been willing to believe anything.

Chapter 8

Next day, Mum went out to ride the ponies with Emily straight after breakfast.

Before long they were back in the kitchen again, red-faced and out of breath.

"I think we may need some help. Lady doesn't seem too keen on the idea of being caught," Mum said. She went to the fridge, took out a couple of carrots and started to chop them up. "Lightning's friendly enough. We've taken her to the gate several times, but Lady doesn't want to know. A little bit of bribery may do the trick."

The whole family marched back to the field, armed with a pink bucket containing orange carrot pieces.

I hope horses really are colour blind, Joe thought.

Lightning came up immediately, and was rewarded with a piece of carrot, and then another. She didn't mind having her head collar put on at all, even though Emily made a complete hash of it the first time and tried to put it on back-to-front. Meanwhile, Lady mooched around in the background, eating grass.

Dad and Emily held Lightning while Mum took the bucket of carrots in one hand, hid the head collar behind her back with the other and walked purposefully towards Lady, who carried on grazing until she could almost touch her, then lifted her head and trotted away.

"Try taking your hat off," Dad called. "She can see you want to ride her."

Mum left her hat on the ground. It didn't seem to make any difference. Lady wasn't going to be caught, end of story.

They tried everything, even cornering her with a length of rope, but she always escaped at the last moment.

"Was she okay about being caught when you went to try her out?" Dad asked.

"Already in a stable," Mum replied breathlessly. "Never crossed my mind she'd be difficult like this."

Dad sighed. "Oh Jackie! *And* you took her head collar off last night!"

"That's right, blame me for everything!" Mum exclaimed.

They started quarrelling about who'd decided to take the head collars off, whether Lady would have been easier to catch if she were wearing one and why Mum hadn't asked more questions about her. Joe hated it when they argued. Emily looked miserable too. Even Lightning was beginning to look upset.

Lightning, Joe thought. "How about—"

"Be quiet, Joe. We're trying to work out what to do," Dad said.

"But—"

"Joe, not now!"

"Why don't we take Lightning out of the field?" Joe said quickly.

Silence. "That's not a bad idea, you know," Mum said.

"Worth a try," Dad admitted.

Dad and Emily led Lightning out of the field and away towards the stables. Joe shut the gate behind them and stood there with Mum. Lady instantly ran to the gate, practically begging to be caught so she could follow her friend.

Joe picked up the head collar and slipped it gently over Lady's nose. Then, with one deft movement, he carefully slid his hand under her cheek, looped the long strap behind her ears and buckled it on his side. He did it instinctively, without really thinking. "Good girl," he murmured. "See, that wasn't so bad, was it?"

"Thank goodness for that," said Mum. "You're a genius, Joe Williams."

Joe spent what was left of the morning helping Dad paint the spare room. Painting wasn't a bad job, and Dad always let him decide what music they had, although he complained if Joe turned it up too loud.

The talk at lunch time was all about the new ponies. Mum and Emily had been riding them around "the estate", as Dad jokily called it, for most of the morning. Emily was insufferable, boasting about her perfect pony and how well she could ride.

She carried on bragging after lunch, while Mum and Dad were outside talking to a man who was installing a TV satellite dish.

"Oh, for goodness sake!" Joe erupted, unable to bear it a moment longer. "Even a baby can walk around on a leading rein, you know."

Emily's face shrivelled with rage. "You're just jealous because you haven't got a pony!" she yelled. "You don't know *anything*!" She stormed out of the back door.

Off to tell Mum I've been horrid to her, I expect, Joe thought. Now I'll be in for another lecture. He took his mobile and headed for the door. He'd go up the road and phone Rahul – see if he'd like to come and stay. It'd be good to see a friendly face.

Through the kitchen window he saw Mum and Dad standing at the front of the house, looking at a man up a ladder drilling holes in the side of the house for a satellite dish. Mum had her hands over her ears in an attempt to block out the sound of the drill. Judging by her expression, she could still hear it.

Joe went through the back door, his mind full of all the things he wanted to tell Rahul. Almost immediately, though, he sensed something was wrong.

Lady and Lightning were charging around the field together, and through the overgrown hedge Joe occasionally glimpsed a small, pink person clinging onto Lightning's back. She was screaming, but he could barely hear it above the noise at the front of the house and the thudding hooves in the field. Emily was screaming, and for once it was justified – even if it wasn't helping the situation one little bit.

Joe looked at the house, then at the field. It'd take too long to go and get Mum and Dad. He ran towards the ponies, stumbling through the long grass. Lightning didn't have any tack on – not even a head collar – and Emily wasn't wearing a riding hat. What on earth had she been thinking of? "Hang on, Emily!" he said under his breath. "Just hang on somehow."

By the time Joe reached them, Emily had stopped screaming and the ponies had slowed down. Lightning limped noticeably, nodding her head with every stride.

Emily's face was pale and rigid with fear. Her small hands clung to Lightning's mane, hanging on desperately as she slid from one side to the other, threatening to go past the point of no return each time.

"Whoa, Lightning," Joe coaxed breathlessly, walking into the field with his arms out.

Lady immediately sprinted to the far end, where she circled around in a high-stepping trot with her tail in the air and a "can't catch me" look on her face. For a dreadful moment Joe thought Lightning might follow, but she didn't. Miraculously, she veered towards him.

"Steady, girl." It sounded like the right sort of thing to say.

Lightning seemed to understand. She walked for a few strides and then stopped, breathing heavily, her dilated nostrils tinged red.

Terrified she might suddenly shy away again, Joe edged round to her side, moving carefully and repeating "Steady, girl, steady." His left hand grasped Emily's leg.

Lightning stood still, her flanks rising and falling as she gradually got her breath back.

Joe was struggling to get his breath back too. Keeping his hand on Emily's leg, he moved closer and put his right arm around her slim little body. "It's okay, I've got you now. You can let go."

Emily didn't move.

"Emily, let go of the mane and I'll lift you off. You're safe now. Come on, fall towards me."

She sat there, motionless.

Using his left hand, Joe carefully uncurled her stiff fingers from their vice-like grip on Lightning's mane, and pulled her off into his arms.

She neither resisted nor helped. It was as if her brain had completely shut down.

He sat her on the ground, kneeling beside her so he could support her back. "Do something, Emily," he said, panic taking a hold now the crisis was over. "Please say something – anything – to let me know you're okay."

"I rode prop-ly," she whispered, then burst into tears.

For once Joe didn't mind Emily crying. At least it proved she was alive. Her bawling gradually subsided into sobs followed by long, shivery breaths. They sat with their arms round each other, feuds temporarily forgotten. Lightning wandered off, tail swishing, to graze in the dazzling sunshine. The drama of a few minutes ago seemed unreal, like waking from a nightmare to find all was well.

Eventually Emily said, "I didn't think she'd get up."

"What d'you mean?" Joe replied.

"Lightning was sunbathing. She looked so comfy. I went to stroke her, and she didn't move. So I sat on her back, and she didn't mind. So I lay on top of her and hugged her neck. She was so lovely and warm. It was nice. I told her all about our argument, and thinking about it made me angry. I shouted *I hate Joe!* and before I could get off, she was up and moving. I clung on to her neck. It was so scary. Then Lady joined in. We went faster and faster, like a race. I thought I was going to d-die." Emily's chin began to tremble.

"Well, you didn't. You're safe now," Joe said.

Emily looked at him, and sniffed. "Don't tell Mummy, will you? She'll be *furious* with me, 'specially as I wasn't wearing a hat."

Joe felt relieved. If Mum found out, it could backfire on him. Everything had turned out okay, so there was no need for anyone to know. He gave Emily a quick hug. "Okay," he said. "It's our secret."

Chapter 9

"Not more expense!" Dad protested. "How much does shoeing cost?"

"I'm not sure, but it's got to be done. Lady can't be ridden with three shoes on and one off. I don't want her to become lame. 'No foot, no horse,' as they say," Mum replied.

"The horsey world seems to be full of little sayings to suit every occasion," Dad said. "Just remember that money's really tight at the moment."

Mum got up from the breakfast table. She kissed the top of Dad's head. "I know, but this is important.

The farrier's coming at nine-thirty, so we'd better get going. Come on, Emily. We'll go and catch the ponies, shall we?"

"Don't feel very well," Emily whimpered. "Tummy-ache."

"I'm not surprised, the amount of toast you've just eaten," Dad said.

"I'll come," Joe said.

Mum smiled. "Thanks, darling. It's so much easier with two people."

"It's lucky we've got Lightning. Without her, Lady would be impossible to catch," she said a few minutes later as they led the ponies into the yard. "That sounds like the farrier now."

A white van drew up, and a slim man dressed in jeans and a singlet got out. "Good morning. It's going to be hot again, by the looks of it," he said. "I'm Chris – Chris Collins."

"Nice to meet you, Chris. I'm Jackie Williams, and this is my son, Joe."

Joe shook Chris's hand. "You ride past our house most days, don't you?"

"Yes, that's my other life – exercising Richard's horses for him. I point-to-point them for him too."

"Who's Richard?" Mum asked.

"Richard Cox. He owns Lucketts Farm. Have you met him yet?"

"No, I don't believe we have."

Joe kept quiet.

"I see you brought your horses with you. Good to have some old friends around when you move house, isn't it?" Chris said. He looked from Lady to Lightning and back again, his gaze lingering on their hooves.

"Actually I've only just bought them," Mum said.

"Oh, right," Chris's face gave nothing away.

He picked up each of Lady's hooves in turn. "Have you got the shoe that fell off?"

"I'm afraid not. We spent ages looking for it in the field, didn't we Joe? It must be in there somewhere. Is it a problem? I mean, could it be dangerous?"

"Well, it could do some damage if they step on it and the nails are pointing upwards," Chris replied. Don't worry too much, though. The countryside must be littered with old horseshoes. It's a wonder so few are found." He patted Lady's broad rump. "Okay, then. Three refits and a new shoe."

Mum looked taken aback. "Oh, I was hoping you'd just do the one that's missing."

"Up to you, but the others definitely need doing. Her hooves are much too long and the shoes are loose."

"How much will it cost?" Mum asked. Chris told her, and she winced. "Well, I suppose there's no point

61

in having a pony if I can't ride her," she said. "I'll have to break it to my husband gently."

Chris walked to the back of the van again. There was a dull whooshing sound.

"What's that noise?" Joe asked.

"A portable forge. Runs off propane gas," Chris replied.

"Is that where you heat up the shoes?"

"That's right. It's revolutionised our job, for sure. In the old days you had to take your horse to the farrier to be shod, but now we can come to you." Chris reached into the side door of the van, and brought out an anvil on a metal stand.

"Why? I mean, why do the shoes have to be hot? Why can't you put them on cold?"

Chris picked up one of Lady's shod hooves, and started to loosen the nails. "You *can* put shoes on cold, but with the steel ones, which most people use, you get a much better fit if you work them when they're hot. Racehorse shoes are usually put on cold, though. They're made out of aluminium, so they can be shaped without heating." He pulled the shoe off, and moved onto the next.

"So why aren't all horseshoes made out of aluminium? Wouldn't that be easier?"

"Not really. Aluminium's lighter but it's not as hard-wearing as steel."

"Don't hot shoes hurt the horse's hoof?"

"No. You see, a hot shoe's only offered up to the hoof, so you can judge if it fits okay. You cool it down before nailing it into place. I'll show you if you stay around."

Chris trimmed Lady's hooves, then chose the right size of shoe from a collection in the back of his van.

"Why do these have ten nail holes in them?" Joe asked. "I thought they were supposed to have seven."

"Ah, traditional hand-made shoes usually have seven holes – four on the outside of the hoof and three on the inside – but most shoes nowadays are machine-made, with symmetrical nail holes already stamped into them. I hardly ever use ten, but there's a good choice of holes here, so I can put nails into the best position on each hoof."

"Like ready-made shelving, with lots of different settings to choose from," said Mum. "I can't help feeling it's cheating, though. I mean, I thought farriers were supposed to make all their own shoes."

Joe winced. Mum could be awfully like a bossy schoolteacher – probably because she was one.

Chris seemed unperturbed. "I can make some from scratch if you like, but they'll be more expensive."

"No, no! That's fine," Mum said quickly. Then, to Joe's relief, she went inside to get on with her work.

"Are horseshoes lucky?" Joe asked as soon as she was out of earshot.

"Supposed to be," Chris replied as he trimmed Lady's foot with a sharp blade. A thick, curved piece of hoof fell to the ground. He glanced up, grinning. "If so, I should be one of the luckiest blokes around, with all those horseshoes in the back of my van." He carried on working. "There is something fairly magical about them, though, and they're one of the few things which have remained pretty well the same for centuries. Fire, metal, horses – they can be traced back into the mists of time, can't they? They're considered lucky in lots of different cultures, too. All I know for certain is I love my work, and not many people can say that, so as far as I'm concerned horseshoes are lucky."

"Do you know a lady called Nellie Reeve?" Joe asked.

Chris chuckled. "Ah! What's she been telling you?"

Joe felt himself blushing. "Nothing much."

"She's fairly eccentric and a bit of a loner, but there's nothing wrong with that. Some people avoid her because she's a gypsy, but I like her."

"Nellie isn't a gypsy, she's a Romany," Joe said. "And she's really interesting. She knows all sorts of things about ..." He hesitated, aware he may be saying too much, and was relieved when Chris cut the conversation short by going to the furnace, taking out a shoe and working it on the anvil. The noise made talking impossible.

Joe stayed, watching. Everything about the process was fascinating: the horses, the tools, the fire, the sweet-smelling smoke, the precision of the work and the musical rhythm of the hammer as the shoe was shaped on the anvil.

There was so much more to it than Joe had realised. Even the nails were complicated, with different parts called the head, neck, shank and point. Chris showed him how the points of the nails were bevelled, or sloping, on the inner surface, and explained that they had to be driven into the hoof with the bevel on the inside, so the point would turn away from the sensitive inner part and emerge from the outer wall in the right place.

"I always thought hooves were solid. I didn't realise there was so much going on in there: bones and nerves and blood vessels and stuff," Joe said.

"Mm, they're really complicated things. There's a lot to learn before you're allowed to shoe a horse."

"How long does it take to become a blacksmith?" Joe asked.

"Blacksmith or farrier?"

"Is there a difference?"

"Certainly is. Blacksmiths forge iron and make

lots of different things out of it. Anyone can be a blacksmith. Don't get me wrong, good smiths are often highly skilled, but you don't need any qualifications to be one. Farriers have to learn blacksmithing together with a whole lot of other things. Only qualified farriers are allowed to shoe horses."

"How d'you become a farrier, then?"

"Lots of hard work," Chris said, placing Lady's forefoot on an iron tripod. "The apprenticeship takes about four years, and you have to learn loads of theory as well as doing all the practical stuff." He turned over the clenches on Lady's hoof, using a hammer and a pair of pincers.

"Four years!" Joe said in amazement. "How old do you have to be to start?"

"Sixteen. I started my apprenticeship when I was seventeen and qualified at twenty-one. I'm twenty-four now, but you never stop learning."

When Chris had finished turning over the clenches, he smoothed them off with a file, working in quick, sure strokes. Finally, he lowered Lady's hoof to the ground and stood upright, stretching his back.

Right on cue, Mum came out with some mugs of tea.

"No sugar, thanks," Chris said as Mum offered him some. "I have to watch my weight for racing."

Mum looked amazed. "But you're so thin!"

"Chris smiled. "But bordering on heavy. I've grown too tall, you see." He took a long sip from his mug. "Now, what do you want me to do about the pony?"

"Oh, nothing," Mum said. "She's just a companion, really – for my daughter to potter around on. She's incurably lame because there's something wrong with her feet. It begins with N, I think."

"Navicular syndrome I expect, judging by the way she's standing. And those shoes, with a rolled toe and raised heels, are often put on animals with navicular. How much do you know about the pony's history and the diagnosis of her problem? Has she had a scan or nerve blocks?"

"I haven't got a clue. All I know is her lameness has become more noticeable in the few days we've had her, which is rather worrying.

"Are you giving her bute?"

"No, I don't even know what it is."

"It's a pain killer – pretty effective too. I expect she was given it at her old home and it's worn off now.

"Oh. Where can I buy it? Have you got some?"

"No, you'll have to get it from a vet, I'm afraid," Chris said. He ran his hand down Lightning's foreleg. "Let's have a look at you, old girl." He whistled through his teeth. "Ouch."

"What's wrong?" Mum asked.

67

"Pretty well everything: long toes, poor digital cushion, almost non-existent frog, under-run heels and a touch of laminitis too, by the looks of it."

"I've heard of laminitis. Isn't that when ponies become lame because they're too fat?"

"Mm, fat ponies are prime candidates, but no horse or pony is immune, especially at this time of year."

"Why? What else causes it?"

"How long have you got? It's a pretty complex subject," Chris replied. "Basically, lots of different things can act as a trigger: too much work on hard ground, long hooves, a hormone imbalance or toxins, for instance. By far the most common cause, though, is too many carbohydrates from grazing rich grass."

"Goodness!" Mum exclaimed. "I had no idea."

Chris stroked Lightning's shoulder. "Anyway, these shoes need to come off before they fall off. Do you want me to make up some more? It's a specialist job and fairly pricey, but I can do it, no problem."

Mum looked horrified. "Oh dear, we really can't afford it. If I'd known Lightning was going to cost a lot to keep I wouldn't have agreed to have her."

Chris looked at the other feet. "Well, if you don't want her shod, there's only one other option: I'll take her shoes off and we'll see how she goes. There's research going on at the moment that suggests if horses suffering from navicular go barefoot and are given the right food and exercise they sometimes come right. If you're prepared to give it a go I'd be really interested to see whether it works."

"Yes, that's a good idea," Mum said, looking relieved.

"It would be a great help if you could stop her from grazing outside when the sun's shining. Sugar levels in the grass are particularly high then," Chris continued. "In fact, if you can keep both horses stabled during the day for the rest of the summer, it'll do their hooves no end of good. They'll need some bedding, of course, and hay to eat."

Mum sighed. "Hay and bedding, you say? I hoped we wouldn't need to buy either for a while. More expense!"

"Afraid so," Chris said. "Horses aren't cheap to keep, that's for certain."

Chapter 10

Emily didn't want to go for a ride the following day. She said she was worried Lightning's feet would be sore without shoes on.

At first, Mum praised Emily for being so considerate towards her pony, and she went for short rides around the fields on Lady by herself. She always looked flustered afterwards, and she told Joe that riding Lady by herself wasn't much fun because she was stubborn going away and unstoppable coming back. "Don't tell Dad, though," she said. "He'll only say 'I told you so'. I'll sort it out somehow.

She just needs firm handling, that's all."

It all came to a head on the day of Joe's first aikido lesson.

As they were eating lunch, Mum said, "Let's go for a ride this afternoon, Emily. I'm sure Lightning will be fine. She doesn't seem as lame as she was, especially now she's getting bute every day, and some gentle exercise will do her good."

"I've got a tummy ache," Emily said.

"You seem to be getting an awful lot of tummy aches recently. Perhaps we ought to go and see a doctor."

"No!" Emily shouted, and started to cry.

"What's wrong, Pumpkin? Don't you like your pony any more? She's in the stable all day, but you never go and see her. What's happened?"

Emily flung herself into Mum's arms, still crying, without any explanation.

I'm going to have to say something, Joe thought. But how can I without getting us both into trouble? Perhaps I should offer to ride Lightning, just to take the pressure off Emily for a while. I wouldn't mind riding again; it'd be something to do. In fact, I'd like to ... He was just about to suggest it when a car drove into the yard.

"Looks as if you're lift's arrived," Dad said. "Have a good time at aikido."

"Bye, darling. Have fun," Mum said. "And remember to thank Nigel for the lift."

Joe picked up his sports bag and went out to the waiting car without a word, wishing his parents would stop organising his life for him. He would have preferred it if Dad had taken him – especially for the first time – and he wanted to be able to choose his own friends.

Nigel, Martin's dad, talked a lot. He chatted away to Joe and Martin as if they were fellow adults. With Joe's parents there was always an invisible barrier, a mental adjustment they made when talking to anyone of school age, even their own children. Perhaps it was because they were teachers.

"Coming to the pub quiz on Wednesday evening?" Nigel asked. "Your dad said he wanted to."

How do I get out of this one? Joe thought. Pub quizzes are for middle-aged geeks who spend ages swotting up facts and figures. Rahul and John would split their sides laughing if I told them I was going to a pub quiz. It's the dead opposite of cool.

"You've got room on your team, Martin, haven't you?" Nigel said.

"Yeah. Several people are away on holiday, so it'd be great if you could come."

"Martin's pretty good, you know. His team often wins the junior prize," Nigel said.

What's the prize? Joe thought. A balloon or something, I bet. No way am I going to get involved in this. "Er, thanks, but I think I'm having to babysit my little sister," he said. He'd never been asked to babysit Emily in his life.

"Bring her along too," Martin said. "She can join our team."

No! Joe wanted to shout. "Thanks, I'll see," he said.

The car pulled in to the side of Bellsham High Street, and Nigel dropped off the two boys, saying he had to go to the cash and carry but he'd park the car and come to the dojo to pick them up.

As they walked along the pavement, Martin said, "It's my birthday on Thursday. Do you want to come over?"

Joe imagined turning up at the pub and finding he was the only person invited. They'd eat chips and watch a DVD or something, and then Martin would think they were best buddies.

How do I get out of this politely? I know! Rahul's coming to stay, he thought. "Thanks, but I can't," he said. "I've got a friend coming to stay."

"Bring him along too. The more the merrier."

Oh blimey, he really is desperate, Joe thought. "Er, I couldn't bring him. It's against his religion to go into a pub." Nothing was further from the truth – Rahul's dad owned a whole chain of them.

"Oh, okay," Martin said. "Poor bloke. What religion's that, then?"

There was a sound of running feet behind them. Two boys ran up and bashed into Martin, then tried to trip him up.

Joe froze, torn between helping Martin and keeping out of trouble.

Martin fended off his attackers easily, a broad grin on his face.

"You win," said the taller boy. "Coming to aikido? Who's your friend?"

I'm not . . . Joe thought.

"Joe," said Martin.

"Hi, Joe. I'm Darren."

"And I'm Spike," said the smaller boy.

They seem good fun, Joe thought. The sort of people I'd like to have as friends. He smiled and said, "Hi."

"Hey, Martin," Darren said. "We're looking forward to the mega-party, aren't we, Spike? Pub quiz on Wednesday and a party on Thursday – ideal! I can't believe you've invited so many people. The whole school seems to be coming, you know. The field will be full of tents again – it was like a pop festival last year, wasn't it? Your parents are mad, but we all love 'em." He looked at Joe. "Oh, sorry. I didn't think. I mean, have you been . . ."

"Don't worry, I invited Joe, but he can't come," Martin said, turning into a side street. Ahead was a building with some Japanese writing and the words *Bellsham Martial Arts School* above the door.

"Why ever not? You'd better have a pretty good reason for missing Martin's birthday party! They've always been awesome, ever since we were little kids," Darren said.

"I've got a friend staying," Joe said lamely.

"And it's against his friend's religion to go into a pub," Martin added.

They started climbing the stairs to the dojo.

"Oh. What religion's that, then?" Darren asked, echoing Martin's question.

Joe pretended he hadn't heard. They knew it was a lie. He'd only dig himself a deeper hole. He pounded up the stairs two at a time.

A girl stood by the entrance to the dojo, dressed in a white gi, or training uniform, with a blue belt around her waist.

"Hi. What are you doing here?" Joe asked, feeling foolish and out of breath.

"Same as you, I expect," Caroline replied. "Having an aikido lesson?"

*

There were eight boys and three girls in the class. The sensei, or instructor, was a charismatic young man with deep green-blue eyes which locked onto Joe's with unnerving intensity when he spoke to him. It took courage to hold his gaze.

Joe didn't like the feeling of being the new boy. He tried his hardest to impress everyone. He was paired with Martin, who was astonishingly good at aikido, which didn't help Joe's feelings of insecurity at all.

At the end of the training session they all stood in a line, facing the sensei.

"Today I want to talk about ego," he said. "Caroline, what is ego?"

"Yourself, sort of?" Caroline said shyly.

"That's right. Or to put it another way, ego is a sense of self. Spike, is ego a good or a bad thing?"

"Bad," Spike said with conviction.

"Yes, it can be," the sensei replied. "We all have an ego. It gives us self-knowledge and self-respect, and those are good, in fact they're essential. But ego is dangerous if it becomes out of control. It turns into a bad thing the moment it makes us believe we're something special, or better than the next person. An example of bad ego is the playground bully who enjoys making others unhappy because it makes him, or her, feel powerful. Or it can be more subtle than that. For instance, we may avoid someone not because we dislike them but because we perceive them to be unpopular or unsuccessful, and we want to hang out with the popular, successful set to make us feel good about ourselves. That's bad ego at work." He was looking straight at Joe now. "So we must all learn to keep our egos in check, mustn't we?"

"Yes, Sensei Radford," they chorused.

"Remember, aikido is the way of harmony. It should be used defensively, not aggressively, to bring harmony to confrontational situations. Harmony is achieved only if you and your partner both train honestly to the best of your ability. Aikido should *never* be used to gratify ego. You should strive to be the best you yourselves can be, without worrying about how you measure up against others. Do you understand?"

"Yes, Sensei Radford."

"Excellent. See you all next weekend."

Chapter 11

Joe thanked Nigel for the lift. He walked to the front door, glad to be out of the car. Martin had been much more aloof on the way back. Who could blame him? He'd given Joe the chance to be his friend, gone out of his way to make him feel included, and Joe had thrown it all back in his face.

Nothing's gone right since we moved, Joe thought as he went into the house.

The kitchen door was ajar. The enticing smell of cooked cheese wafted out. He could hear Emily talking, but it wasn't the way she talked to Mum and

Dad. It was the sensible, best behaviour voice she saved for adults she didn't know very well. He pushed the door open, and walked in.

Nellie Reeve and Emily were sitting at the kitchen table.

Before anyone could say anything, Emily got up from her chair, ran over to Joe and stared up at him, wide-eyed with the importance of what she had to say. "Mummy's had an accident!" Excitement and terror mingled together in her voice. "She's in hospital. Daddy's gone too, and we're eating cheese on toast."

The full story gradually came out. Mum had decided to go out for a hack on Lady, leaving Lightning behind in the stable because Emily had refused to ride. Lady had made a terrible fuss, whinnying and trying to return to her friend. Mum had become very cross with her.

A tractor pulling a silage wagon had been rumbling down the road just as Mum and Lady were approaching Orchard Rise. Nellie had been in her garden, so she'd seen the whole thing. Lady had panicked, spun round and bolted for home, leaving Mum lying on the tarmac, unconscious. An ambulance had taken Mum to hospital, and Nellie had offered to stay at Newbridge Farm with Emily and Joe, so Dad could be with Mum.

It was hard to take it all in. "Is she okay? Have you heard anything?" Joe asked.

"I hope she'll be fine. It was a nasty fall, but the ambulance came quickly," Nellie replied. "And no, we haven't heard anything yet, but the trouble is there's no landline connection and no mobile signal here. I've given your dad my telephone number, so after you've had some tea we'll let the ponies out into the field and then go up to my house to wait for news."

"I'm not hungry," Joe said. "Let's go now."

They all walked over to the stables together. It felt unreal. Mum had always been there – organising, cooking, cleaning, comforting, lecturing, encouraging, turning up to every football match to cheer Joe on – sometimes annoying, often embarrassing, but always there. He felt as if his whole life was teetering on the edge of a precipice. How would they all cope if she didn't recover? It was unthinkable.

Lady whinnied as they came close, apparently unaware of the damage she'd done.

She's only pleased to see us because she wants to be let out so she can eat grass, Joe thought. He couldn't even bear to look at her, the pig-headed, ugly brute.

"I'll take this one and you can take the chestnut," Nellie said, fitting Lady's head collar with the ease of someone who'd done it so many times she could do it by feel alone.

Emily lingered in the background.

"Do you want to help me, Emily?" Nellie asked.

"No thanks," she replied.

Lightning bent her head round towards Joe, practically begging to have her head collar put on. You should have been called Lady, he thought. It would have suited you.

Lady, as usual, barged out of her stable and rushed towards the nearest patch of grass, her thick neck braced solid.

"Oh no you don't," Nellie said, standing still and pulling her round.

In an instant Lady was facing her.

Nellie walked forwards. "Back! Back up!" she said sternly.

Lady looked surprised, but she backed up.

Nellie led her around the yard a few times, making her stop, back up and turn in circles. After a few minutes they were moving so easily together it looked like dancing.

"What a good girl," Nellie said. "She's a quick learner."

Joe knew he was scowling, but he couldn't help it. How could she say Lady was a good girl when she so obviously hadn't been?

"You can't blame her for what's happened, Joe," Nellie said, guessing his thoughts. "Lord knows what she's been through in her life, but it's destroyed her faith in human nature. The slightest thing tips her off balance."

What on earth's she going on about? Joe wondered.

"She's learned she can't trust people, so she tries to ignore them and make her own decisions," Nellie went on. "Of course, that wouldn't really be a problem if she were a wild horse living with other horses, but she's in a human world which she doesn't understand."

"Why was she so good when she was shod the other day, then?" Joe asked.

"She's probably never had a bad experience with a farrier," Nellie said. "Just proves how generous she is. She takes people as she finds them, gives everyone a chance." She stroked Lady's neck as the pony stood quietly by her side, completely relaxed. "Chris shod her, didn't he?"

Joe nodded.

"He's got good energy," she said. "Horses pick up on that."

"What's good energy?" Joe asked. It sounded like renewable electricity.

"Good energy is calm, confident, controlled energy, like you're taught to have in aikido."

How does she know about that? Joe wondered.

"Balance and focus are both important in aikido, aren't they?" Nellie went on.

Joe nodded. He'd heard it said often enough, but he and his friends had started aikido in the hopes they'd be able to defend themselves against the school bullies, not for any deep spiritual reasons.

"You see," Nellie explained, "when we're calm and in balance we can see things clearly, like looking into a still pond. But when we're frightened, angry or excited we're out of balance and we can't see clearly, like looking into a pond with lots of ripples running over it. Horses seem to know how dangerous it is to be out of balance, and they try their hardest to avoid it."

Joe was beginning to see what she meant, sort of.

"Think what you feel like when your parents are cross with you."

Joe thought.

"It's especially bad if you think it's unfair and they don't understand, isn't it?"

Joe smiled, and nodded, thinking of the day he'd dug up the horseshoe.

"Upsets you, doesn't it? Throws you off balance?"

"Yes."

"So imagine what Lady felt like. The tractor was

83

just the final straw in a long chain of events which threw her off balance so she couldn't think straight. Instinct took over, and she fled back to safety. She didn't mean to hurt your mum. She was just being a horse."

Chapter 12

Nellie's house was every bit as extraordinary as Joe had thought it would be. Each room was tiny, but crammed full of treasures: china, silver, brass, models of horses and wagons, ornaments and photos. One particular photo caught his eye. It was of a vardo pulled by a piebald horse.

"Molly taking us to Appleby Fair," Nellie said. "Dear old Molly."

Joe studied the photo. "It must be fun travelling like that – and living in a vardo. What are they like inside?"

Nellie smiled as she remembered. "Ours was so

cosy, with everything you could possibly need: cupboards, seats, a stove and a pull-out bed."

The telephone rang, making them all jump. Nellie answered it.

"Oh, right ... Well, that's something ... Yes, only to be expected ... Of course not ... Yes, fine ... Don't worry, I'll tell them ... No need to hurry. Bye." Nellie put the phone down.

Joe and Emily stared at her silently. A clock ticked on the mantelpiece. Joe wondered why he hadn't heard it before.

"Your mum's conscious, but she's hurt herself quite badly, "Nellie said. "She's broken some ribs and a collar bone, and she's got severe concussion. She'll have to stay in hospital for a while."

Emily looked worried. "What's can-cushion?"

Nellie didn't correct her, as Mum would have done. She just said, "It's when your brain becomes bruised and sore because you've had a bang on the head."

"Oh. She'll be okay, won't she?"

"Well, it sounds as if she's making good progress, but it'll take time," Nellie said. "Your dad says he's coming back now. What would you like to do while we're waiting?"

Emily pointed to the TV in the corner of the room. "Can we watch *Fame and Fortune*?"

"Sure, help yourself," Nellie said, handing her the

remote control. "I'll be outside in the garden if you need me."

Joe tried to watch *Fame and Fortune*, but the glamour, glitz and synthetic smiles made a mockery of what was happening in his world – the real world where there was nothing to smile about. Leaving Emily cuddling Mittens, the cat, he went outside. Nellie was collecting eggs from the chicken ark.

"I'll give you some to take back with you," she said. "I always have far too many at this time of year."

"Thanks," Joe said.

It started to rain. Warm, fat drops stippled the parched ground.

"This'll do the plants some good," Nellie said, shutting the door to the chicken ark. "Have you still got that horseshoe?"

Joe was taken by surprise. "Er, yes. It's under my bed at the moment, in a box of clothes. I didn't have any coloured paper, you see."

"I've got some, if you want," Nellie said. "But don't feel you have to do anything. The moment's got to be right."

"I wasn't sure what my wishes would be," Joe said. "But I think I know now. Have you got a candle I can borrow as well?"

"Of course. Let's take these eggs into the kitchen, and I'll see what I can find."

*

It was a wonder that Nellie managed to find anything. Her kitchen, like the rest of her house, was stuffed full of possessions.

"I don't throw anything away if I can help it. You never know what may come in handy someday," she said, rummaging around in a cupboard. A huge stack of old egg boxes toppled out and scattered over the floor. She picked one up. "See? We'll need one of those for your eggs!"

Joe retrieved the rest and re-built a tower of them in the cupboard. Meanwhile, Nellie gathered the things he'd need for his wishing shoe into a carrier bag.

Soon Dad arrived. "I don't know how to thank you enough," he said.

"They were no problem," Nellie replied. "I enjoyed the company."

Emily gave Nellie a hug. "Thank you!" she said. Nellie looked pleased.

Joe wasn't sure whether to hug Nellie, shake her hand or just thank her. He stood there, feeling awkward.

Nellie smiled. "Bye, Joe. I'll come over at eight tomorrow morning, to help you with the ponies."

"Okay, thanks very much," he replied.

Chapter 13

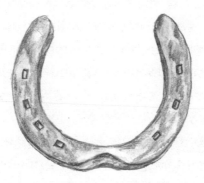

That night, after supper, when Emily was in bed and Dad was downstairs watching the TV, Joe unpacked the plastic bag Nellie had given him: a red candle in a candlestick, matches, coloured paper, a pair of pliers and some sandpaper.

Getting the bent, encrusted nails out of his horseshoe was much more difficult than he'd expected. The pliers slipped several times, bashing into his hands, and some of the nails broke off in jagged fragments. Even when they were all out, the task of sanding down the shoe lay ahead.

"This had better be worth it," Joe said to himself, shredding his fingers as well as the sandpaper as he tried to rub the rust off the shoe and into the bin. Fine orange-brown dust settled on his clothes and hands.

"That'll have to do," he said finally as the last bit of sandpaper fell to pieces, worn out by friction. The shoe was still rusty, but at least it now looked like a proper horseshoe, complete with a toe clip at the front, four nail holes on one branch and three on the other.

With a tingle of excitement, Joe lit the candle on his desk. He'd never done anything like this before. It felt crazy and slightly spooky. The golden flame flickered, then grew tall and strong. He turned out the electric light. The room softened in the candle's orange glow, fading away into darkness at the edges. Rain pattered against the window.

He took a crumpled piece of paper from his pocket, sat down at the table and read what he'd written in Nellie's kitchen: *green = money, blue = health, red = employment, purple = friendship, yellow = spiritual, orange = legal, brown = home, white = everything else.*

Although he'd been thinking of wishes all evening, it was difficult to remember them now. He sorted out the coloured pieces of paper, and found a pen.

After a brief pause, he wrote *I hope Mum gets better very soon* on a square of blue paper. The paper was quite stiff. He curled it up as tightly as he could, but it wouldn't fit into the narrow nail hole. Tearing it in half, he tried again, but it still wouldn't fit. This is hopeless, he thought, tearing it again. I really need scissors, but that'll mean going downstairs and asking Dad for some. I'll just have to be as careful as possible . . .

Eventually he managed to get a rolled up piece of paper no bigger than a large postage stamp through the hole. His wishes would have to be short.

Get well Mum he wrote in the smallest, neatest writing he could manage. Then he rolled the tiny scrap of blue paper up again and stuffed it through the hole. One down, six to go.

Brown paper next, for the wish that had been top of his list ever since they'd left Birmingham. *Go home*, he wrote, and pushed the rolled up paper through the next hole.

In Birmingham he and his friends had been in and out of each other's houses the whole time. He missed that so much. What should he wish for? To keep his old friends – and make some new ones as well, in case his family were stuck here for a while? His thoughts had too many words in them, so he simply put *Friends* on some purple paper.

After a moment's thought, he smiled to himself and wrote *My own dog* on some more purple paper.

He rolled them both up. Now all four holes on the outside of the shoe had slim notes sticking out of them.

What next? He'd thought of wishing for fame and fortune while Emily had been watching *Fame and Fortune* on the TV in Nellie's house. A fortune would mean Mum and Dad would never have to work again. They wouldn't get stressed about money the whole time, and they'd all be able to live where they wanted to and do as they pleased. Ideal. What would it really be like to be famous, though? Some celebrities had a terrible time if people suddenly turned against them, didn't they? How awful for that to happen. It would be like being bullied at school but a zillion times worse.

Perhaps it would be better to be something else rather than famous. Good at aikido? Good at football? Good at saying the right thing? Good at making friends? His mind kept settling on the word *good*. He remembered what Nellie had said about good energy. That would cover most things, wouldn't it? He liked the idea. It sounded fun and powerful and, well, good.

He wrote *Fortune* on a piece of green paper, and *Good energy* on some yellow paper because he thought it counted as spiritual.

One more. I'd love a really expensive bike, Joe thought. But with a fortune I'll be able to buy whatever

I want, won't I? What else? I know! How about playing for England? Wouldn't that just be so cool? I'll put it down as a sort of wild card. Then, if it happens, I'll know this whole wishing thing has worked.

He wrote *England team* on a white note. Crazy, but why not? No harm in trying.

He rolled up the green, yellow and white bits of paper and stuck one through each of the remaining holes in the horseshoe. It looked most peculiar, like a novelty matchstick holder or a wacky piece of modern art. Well, he'd gone this far, so he may as well see it through. He placed the horseshoe in a box, put that inside the large cardboard box containing clothes and covered it with some more clothes. "Kushti bok," he whispered as he closed the lid and hid it under his bed again.

Now all he had to do was wait and see.

Chapter 14

Several things happened, good and bad, in the week after the accident, but nothing that could be described as a wish come true. Newbridge Farm finally had a telephone and internet connection, Mum came out of hospital – needing peace and quiet and a lot of care – Rahul's visit had to be cancelled and several neighbours they'd never met properly before called in with gifts and good wishes. Joe escaped out of the back door when Richard Cox and his wife came, hoping Richard wouldn't say anything about the silage bales. He didn't, and Mum and Dad said afterwards what nice people they were.

Every morning and evening Nellie turned up without fail to help Joe with the ponies, and he began to look forward to it. Lady and Lightning gave him something worthwhile to do. He spent hours happily pottering around the stables during the day, discovering a calm contentment he'd never known before through little things like the rhythmic chomping of a pony eating hay, the smell and suppleness of the neglected tack after he'd rubbed a whole can of harness oil into it, or the sleepy pleasure on Lightning's face as he sifted through the golden hairs in her tail and gently teased out any tangles. He even enjoyed sorting out Lady's thick tail and sponging away the greeny-brown stains which had accumulated on the white parts of her body. After a while both ponies shone with health and regular grooming.

"Fit for the show ring, the pair of them," Nellie commented. She nodded towards Lightning. "Especially that one. She's something special, and no mistake."

"It's no good," Dad said one breakfast time a few days after Mum came out of hospital. "Those ponies will have to go back."

Joe stopped eating. "What d'you mean? Go back where?"

"To Mrs Peters, of course. It's obvious she lied about Lady. She was sold as a quiet hack, but she's nothing of the sort, and now we're lumbered with two useless creatures that can't be ridden and cost a small fortune to keep. I've looked up the Sales of Goods Act, and this is a clear case of misrepresentation."

"What's mis-present-ation?" Emily chipped in.

"*Misrepresentation* is when a seller makes false statements about something they want someone else to buy," Dad said.

"You mean lies?" Emily asked, eyes wide with astonishment.

"Yes, to put it bluntly. Mrs Peters told Mum things that weren't true about Lady, so Mum and I have decided she'll have to take the ponies back and give us a refund."

"But ... They can't go back, not now ... I mean, not now—" Joe's words petered out. He wanted to say something like *not now I've become so fond of them*, but he was afraid it would sound silly. He'd only been caring for them for a few days, after all. He stared at his half-eaten piece of toast, silent and wretched.

"It's no use getting sulky, Joe," Dad said. "You've had fun playing around with the ponies for a week or two, but you'll soon get bored. We could have gone on a holiday of a lifetime with what we've spent on them, and Mum wouldn't have ended up in hospital."

How dare he? Joe thought. That's so unfair! I won't get bored with them and I haven't been playing! He looked up, defiant now. "How d'you know?"

"Pardon?"

"How d'you know Mum wouldn't have ended up in hospital? People often have accidents on holiday. All sorts of things can—"

"Now you're being ridiculous. You know perfectly well what I mean," Dad said.

"I'll get a holiday job," Joe said quickly. "All the money I earn can go towards the ponies." He knew he was clutching at straws. No holiday job could earn anything like the amount of money he'd need.

Dad's expression softened. "You've become rather attached to them, haven't you?"

He nodded.

Dad sighed. "I'm sorry, Joe. We really can't keep them. But we'll get you that dog you've always wanted just as soon as we can find one, okay?" The tone of his voice told Joe the conversation about the ponies was over.

Okay about the dog, not okay about the ponies, Joe thought, studying his toast again, trying to work out what to say.

"Oh, for goodness sake!" Dad said, exasperated.

"Please don't be so *grumpy*!"

Joe got up and left the kitchen. He felt ... he felt all the things Nellie had said about bad energy. He was out of balance, upset, unable to think straight.

The field was the obvious place to go. As he approached, Lady and Lightning whinnied. He rubbed his eyes, pushing back the tears. Nellie would arrive at any moment, and he didn't want her to see he'd been crying.

He caught both the ponies easily and led them to their stables, a rope in each hand. This was their new life. They had a routine, friendship and kindness, and they were content.

By the time Nellie arrived, Joe had done everything. "I've taught you too well. I'm redundant!" she said. Her expression became serious. "Are you okay?"

"Yes, fine," Joe said, trying to smile.

"Well, you know where to find me if you need me."

"Thanks," Joe said, grateful she'd left it at that. Mum would have kept probing. He wanted to come to terms with the situation before saying anything about it. Saying it would make it real. Every time he thought about the ponies going back to an uncertain future with Mrs Peters, he felt like bursting into tears.

He stayed for a long time after Nellie had gone, grooming and talking to them.

When he finally returned to the house, Dad was

the one looking fed up. He said he'd telephoned Mrs Peters and she'd been very rude.

She'd said Lady had always been fine with her and it wasn't her fault if Mum and Dad were so incompetent they couldn't control her. Mum could easily have asked to see Lady being caught or ridden alone, if those things were important to her, but she hadn't.

So Dad had rung his solicitor, who'd told him the Sales of Goods Act applied when buying from someone classified as a horse dealer but not when buying privately. Mum had been unwise to buy privately if she wasn't experienced, he'd said, because then the law *caveat emptor*, or *let the buyer beware*, applied. Mum hadn't had the horse vetted, hadn't got an adult witness and hadn't asked for anything in writing about the ponies, so her best bet was to sell them at a reduced price or, failing that, to give them away.

"I really don't know what to do," Dad said, sitting at the kitchen table with his head in his hands. "Nobody will want them – not even for free – but I haven't the heart to put them down."

Joe grinned. "Looks like we'll have to keep them, then."

*

"Sorry there's only money inside, but I couldn't get to the shops to buy a proper present," Joe said as he gave Martin a birthday card on the way to aikido the following Saturday. He'd had to choose one from Mum's emergency store of cards, and this was the best of the bunch – or the least awful. It had an idyllic country scene with a vintage tractor in the foreground. He'd never have given any of his old friends a card like that, but it seemed appropriate for Martin.

Martin opened the card. "Wow! Couldn't be better! I desperately need to buy some more fly-tying stuff."

"Some what?"

"You know, things to make flies with. Artificial flies, for fly-fishing."

"Oh, I see!" I can't believe I'm trying to make friends with someone whose hobby's making artificial flies, Joe thought. It's so way out it's actually pretty cool.

Everyone was surprisingly friendly at aikido, even if they did keep on about how fantastic Martin's party had been. At the end of the lesson they all lined up facing Sensei Radford again.

"Can anyone tell me what 'ki' means? Yes, Darren?"

"Energy?"

"Yes, ki means energy, but it's much more than plain energy. Power, speed, timing and rhythm are all a part of ki, and they lead to the mastery of balance.

Think about the movements you've performed today. Were they straight?"

They all shook their heads.

"What shape were they? Yes, Martin?"

"Sort of circular?"

"Correct," Sensei Radford said. "You see, aikido is all about blending with the motion of the attacker so the force of the attack is redirected. Circular movements allow us to redirect power without clashing with it, so the attacker's energy ends up working against him, or her. Any questions? Yes, Caroline?"

"Is that why we use circles a lot when we're riding?"

"What a good question," he said. "I'm afraid I don't know much about horses, but I expect there are a lot of similarities between aikido and horsemanship. For instance, you work in pairs, you need to respect each other and you aim for harmony and balance. Am I right?"

Caroline nodded enthusiastically.

"And because even tiny ponies are much stronger than humans, you need skill more than physical strength to direct their energy ... So yes, I expect circular movements are very important in horsemanship."

Caroline nodded again, and Joe found himself nodding as well.

"Is there anything you'd like to add, Joe?" Sensei Radford asked.

Joe felt himself blush as he became the focus of attention. "I was just thinking about Nellie. She helps me with the ponies, and she stopped our big pony, Lady, from running away to eat grass by standing still and pulling her round. Then she carried on turning her in circles, and after that Lady was really well behaved."

"Excellent, Joe. Thank you," Sensei Radford said. "A perfect example. You see, the principles of aikido relate to everything we do in life, not just what happens here in this dojo. Respect, courage, honour, good manners, focus and concentration are important all the time, aren't they?"

"Yes, Sensei Radford," the whole class replied.

"Through these things we achieve balance and harmony in our lives. Good, we've done a lot today. Thank you for being a pleasure to teach, all of you, and I'll see you next week."

As Joe, Martin, Darren and Spike were leaving the dojo together, Caroline caught up with them.

"I didn't realise you liked horses, Joe," she said. "I thought it was just your sister."

"No, I always have," Joe said, "but people don't

expect boys to be into horses for some reason."

Caroline smiled. She really did have very white teeth. "People don't expect girls to be into aikido or football either, but I am. Sorry I haven't asked Emily to come and see our horses yet, by the way. I meant to drop in and ask her, but there's been so much going on, with Pony Club and everything. How about bringing your ponies up to the farm tomorrow so we can all go for a ride together?"

She made it sound so simple. What a pity it wasn't. "I'm afraid neither of our ponies can be ridden at the moment. Lightning's lame and Lady's, um, a bit loopy, I suppose. My parents have made us promise not to ride her."

"I bet Chris would ride her. He loves a challenge," Caroline said.

"Chris the farrier?"

"Yes. He's my half-brother. Have you met him?"

"Yup, he shod Lady. She seemed to like him."

"All horses like Chris. I'll ask him for you, if you like."

"Thanks."

Caroline put her hand on Joe's arm. It felt strangely tingly. "Tell you what, why don't you come up to the farm with Emily tomorrow anyway? Bring your riding hats, just in case."

I haven't got a riding hat and Emily's become

scared of horses, Joe thought. "Thanks, that'd be great," he said.

A Range Rover pulled up by the side of the road in front of them, and Caroline's dad leaned over to look out of the open passenger window. "Martin, Joe, I'm giving you both a lift. Hop in," he said.

The boys clambered into the spacious back seat while Caroline got into the front.

"It's okay, Martin, nothing's happened. It just seemed silly for your father to come all this way when I was picking up Caroline anyway," Richard Cox said, easing the huge car back into the stream of rush hour traffic. He projected self-confidence. Joe was afraid to speak for fear of saying the wrong thing, and Martin seemed to feel the same.

Caroline, on the other hand, chatted away happily. "How's Rusty?" she asked.

There was a scrabbling and whining noise from the boot of the car, which had purpose-built dog cages fitted into it. Looking over his shoulder as much as his seat belt would allow, Joe could see a black nose poking between the bars.

"Ah, hello, Rusty!" Caroline said.

There was more scrabbling and whining.

"Useless hound," her father said. "It was a total waste of time taking him to David's this afternoon. He was much more interested in playing football with the children than rounding up sheep. So much for buying an expensive puppy with some of the best breeding in the country. I may as well have gone for an unregistered mutt from a local farm."

"Perhaps he'll get to like rounding up sheep when he's older," Caroline suggested.

"Mm, I doubt it, and so does David. He's nearly two, so if he's not keen on being a sheepdog by now he never will be. We'll just have to find him a good home where he can play football, follow horses out on rides and have his tummy scratched for hours on end. That seems to be all he wants out of life."

Joe felt his heart beating a little faster. Say something, he thought, but he remained silent. When he turned to look, the black nose had disappeared.

"I'll have him," said Caroline. "I'll keep him as a pet."

"No, darling. One little terrier creates enough havoc in your bedroom. Heaven help us if you had a great big hairy border collie in there too."

"I'll keep him outside in the kennel."

"And who'd end up looking after him?"

"Okay, you would," Caroline said in a sing-song voice, "but we could keep him as a pet for the whole family, couldn't we? He loves going out with the horses."

"Darling, we've already got two Labs, a sheepdog

and three terriers – that's quite enough – *plus* I'll have to get another sheepdog puppy to train up quickly because Fly will be ready to retire soon. Collies are very active dogs, and highly intelligent. Rusty needs to be doing something, even if he's not rounding up sheep. He'd probably make an excellent search and rescue dog, for instance. David's given me the number of a man who's always looking out for collies to train. Ignoring sheep's a positive advantage in that job, apparently."

I'll have him, I'll have him. Joe played the words over and over in his mind, but nothing came out. Even the name was perfect. Rusty, like the rusty horseshoe in the box under his bed, holding a wish for a dog ... If only he could pluck up the courage to say something ... He would once they'd dropped Martin off ...

They said goodbye to Martin and drove on.

Joe took a deep breath. Now or never, he thought.

"I'm sorry about your mum's accident, by the way," Caroline said, turning her head round towards Joe.

"Yes, how is she?" her dad added.

"Still sore, but getting a bit better every day, I think," Joe replied. There was silence as the car purred through the village, past The Old Post Office, The Old Smithy and The Old Tannery.

They were nearly out of the village now, crossing

the narrow stone bridge ... climbing the hill ...

I'll ask about Rusty when we turn right at the crossroads, Joe decided. Ready, steady –

"Will your parents have any spare fields at Newbridge?" Richard Cox asked, throwing Joe off-course yet again. "If so, I'd be interested in a grass let on a couple of them."

"Um, I don't know," Joe replied. "Mum wanted to have a horse sanctuary when we moved here, but I think she may have been put off horses for a while. Everything's been a bit uncertain since her accident."

"Of course. Well, could you could mention it to them, perhaps?"

The Range Rover was already descending the hill to the new bridge. "If you want to come in, I'm sure they'd like to see you."

"Oh, please do! Then Joe can show me his ponies," Caroline said.

"Well, as long as you're sure your parents won't mind."

"Mum loves visitors," Joe said. Now he'd be able to show Caroline the ponies and ask her about Rusty. Perhaps they'd even be able to let him out for a run.

The Range Rover slowed down and turned left into the drive.

"Oh no, I've just remembered I've got an important meeting this evening. Lots of paperwork to do beforehand," Richard Cox said. "I'm so sorry, but I won't be able to stop after all. Please give your parents my best wishes, Joe. I'll ring them about the grazing."

The car ground to a halt. Joe couldn't believe it. Say something about Rusty, he thought. Silence.

Caroline and her dad both turned round to look at him.

"Er, thank you very much for the lift, Mr Cox," he said quickly. "Bye, Caroline."

"Bye bye, Joe. See you tomorrow. Come after lunch," Caroline said.

"Great. Thanks." He got out reluctantly, catching a glimpse of Rusty in his cage as he shut the car door.

The car moved away, turned and disappeared down the drive.

Chapter 15

J oe hardly slept that night. He had an image in his head that wouldn't go away. It was of a border collie called Rusty who played football and wasn't interested in sheep. What if he'd missed his chance? What if Rusty had already gone by the following afternoon? What if he couldn't pluck up the courage to ask if he could have him? Perhaps Caroline's dad would want a lot of money for him, as he was so well-bred. He hadn't thought about that ... Joe's heart raced and his mind buzzed with anxiety. He hadn't wanted anything so much in all his life. He felt completely worn out when he got up for breakfast.

The morning dragged. He couldn't settle to anything. Mum's riding hat had been thrown away after the accident, Emily's was too small for Joe, and Dad refused to take him to Landsdown Farmers to buy one. It looked as if he'd have to admit he didn't even own a riding hat when they visited Lucketts Farm.

Emily complained she had a tummy ache all morning. She lay curled up on the sofa, watching TV. Joe knew it was because she wanted an excuse not to go to Lucketts Farm. She seemed to have undergone a complete transformation from being pony-mad to pony-averse, and he found himself longing to have the annoying pony-mad Emily back again. As lunch time approached it became clear he'd be visiting Caroline alone, and without a riding hat.

They were just finishing lunch when there was a knock at the door.

Joe answered it, and found Caroline and Chris standing outside.

"Hi," Chris said. "Caroline told me you wanted someone to ride your coloured cob mare, to see whether she's okay?"

"D'you mean now?"

"Well, I've got a couple of hours spare, so it'd be a good opportunity, if you'd like me to."

"Yes, fine, great, thanks," Joe said, trying to sound appreciative when all he could think about was getting to Lucketts Farm as quickly as possible to see Rusty. "Um, come in."

Dad offered Chris and Caroline a cup of tea, which they accepted. They sat down and talked for ages about the weather, Lady and the problems of buying and selling horses.

Mum shifted in her armchair by the range, and winced with pain as she tried to get more comfortable. "I used to think all horses were worth a lot of money, no matter what they were like, but lots can't even be given away for one reason or another – and we've ended up with two of them. It seems my plan of having a sanctuary for horses has started already. The trouble is, though, Lady and Lightning belong to us and we're not getting paid to keep them."

"Mm, it's a real problem, from shaggy little moorland ponies to racehorses," Chris said. "Top-class thoroughbreds, for instance, are worth a small fortune, but the ones who get injured or don't make the grade for some reason are pretty well worthless. Meat money, that's the bottom line, I'm afraid, and a lot aren't even worth that. The trouble is that all horses are expensive to keep."

"Tell me about it," Dad said.

"Anyway, I've been talking too much as usual,"

Chris said. "Let's go and see the ponies, shall we?"

To Joe's amazement, Emily got down from her chair, went to the back door and led the way to the stables.

"This is probably part of your problem," Chris said as he saddled Lady. "Look, it doesn't fit her at all. I bet it pinches here and here . . . here as well, I expect. He took the saddle off again, led her out of her stable by her bridle, put on his hard hat and in one swift, effortless motion jumped onto her back. "Tell you what, I'll be able to work her much better in the indoor school up at Lucketts. Why don't we take both ponies there? Put a head collar on the chestnut, and I'll lead her from this one, if you like."

How lovely to be so confident, Joe thought as he handed him Lightning's lead rope. He looked completely at home sitting on Lady's bare, broad back.

"See you up there, then," Chris said, and set off towards the road.

Lucketts Farm was even more impressive than it had looked from a distance. Everything, from the house to the stables and farm buildings, was huge and immaculate, linked by acres of concrete and carefully landscaped areas of lawn and garden. This was modern farming on an industrial scale – big business at work in the countryside. Joe looked around hopefully for dogs, but couldn't see any.

Chris was already in the indoor school when Joe, Caroline and Emily arrived. It was a massive shed with a soft, sandy surface and heaps of equipment stored at one end: jumps, poles of different colours and sizes, buckets and lots of other things. There were also signs with letters of the alphabet on them fixed at intervals along the walls, like they'd had at the riding school. Joe could still remember his riding teacher shouting things like, "Turn right at A and go straight down the centre line!" and the rhyme they'd been taught to remember the sequence of markers around the outside of the arena: All King Edward's Horses Can Manage Big Fences. Funny what stuck in the mind.

"I really like this chestnut pony of yours," Chris said. "What's she called again?"

"Lightning," Joe said.

"Yes, Lightning's a really nice pony, isn't she? It's a pity about her feet, but they've definitely improved since we took her shoes off. You'll have one classy pony to ride if we can get her sound."

Chris held out Lightning's lead rope. "Can you

hold onto her, Joe? Caroline, go and get Muffin's old saddle from the tack room, will you?"

Caroline went out, and returned carrying a saddle.

"Thought so," Chris said, sliding it into position on Lady's back and studying it from every angle. "That's a hundred times better than the other one. You can borrow this for now, if you like." Even though he now had a saddle with stirrups, he vaulted onto Lady and started riding her round the arena.

"How does he do that?" Joe asked.

"Do what? Ride?" Caroline replied.

"No, jump on like that."

"Oh, vaulting's easy, once you know how," Caroline said. "Chris became really good at it when he was in the Prince Philip Cup. He was in the winning team two years running."

"Wow!" Joe said, knowing he should be impressed but not sure why.

"What's the Prince Philip Cup?" Emily asked. She was definitely useful sometimes.

"Do you know what gymkhana games are?" Caroline asked.

"Yes, we did them when we had fun days at the riding school. Bending races and things."

"Well, in the Pony Club we call those sorts of races mounted games. There's a junior team, which I'm in at the moment, and then an older Prince Philip Cup team for people up to fifteen years old. There are lots of competitions all over the country, and the winners from each area go to the finals at the Horse of the Year Show to compete for the Prince Philip Cup. The Bellsham Vale – that's our Pony Club branch – often gets to the finals. We haven't won for ages, though, not since Chris was in the team.

Chris stopped Lady in the centre of the arena. "Joe!" he called.

Lightning, who'd been standing peacefully at Joe's side, suddenly leapt into action and tried to run forwards. Instinctively, he stood his ground and pulled her round. She turned easily, and stood looking at him, tense with excitement.

"That's odd. I wonder what scared her," Caroline said.

"She does that every now and then," Joe said. "I don't know why. She's usually so good. It's as if a switch flips in her brain."

"Perhaps something's spooked her."

"Mm, perhaps. It happens at home as well, though."

"Yes," Emily chipped in. "The worst time was when I shouted, 'I hate Joe!' Lightning jumped up and galloped off, and I ..." Her words trailed off as she realised she was about to tell the story she wanted to remain a secret.

Caroline giggled. "Sounds as if she's scared of your name, Joe."

"She looks excited rather than frightened, though," he replied, "as if my name's a cue to go fast or something."

Chris dismounted and walked over to them. "I think you've hit the nail on the head. Caroline, can you go and get a lunge line? Hang on to Lady, Joe, and I'll take Lightning a minute. I'd like to try something."

Caroline soon came back with a long coil of soft webbing, which Joe presumed was a lunge line.

Chris attached the clip on the line to Lightning's head collar, led her to the centre of the indoor school and asked her to walk on.

Lightning set off calmly.

Chris gradually let the lunge line out until she was walking in a large circle. "Ready, steady, go!" he said in a loud voice.

Lightning went. Joe had to use all his strength to stop Lady from joining in as she galloped around at the end of the lunge line.

When Chris had slowed her to a walk again, he said softly, "There's your answer. She's learned to respond to the word *go*. *Joe* sounds remarkably similar, of course, so it has the same effect. You've got yourself a racing pony."

"Wow! What sort of races?"

"I've no idea, but I bet she was good. If we can find out, we may be able to discover what happened to her and why she became so lame. The more we know, the greater our chances of helping her to come right."

"D'you think she will? Become completely sound, I mean?"

"I don't see why not. She's so much better already," Chris replied. "Now then, could you take her for a walk outside? I want to see what Lady does without her."

Joe led Lightning outside. The strong sunshine made him squint after the cool shade of the indoor school. No sooner had Caroline closed the door behind them than Lady started making a fuss, whinnying urgently. Lightning gave a couple of half-hearted whinnies in reply, more out of politeness than anxiety.

Joe stroked her neck. "Come on, little racehorse," he said, and led her away towards the house.

Caroline's mum appeared from the garden by the side of the house, holding a small boy by the hand. Three dogs bounded ahead of her: two Labradors and Rusty. Joe knew it was Rusty the moment he saw him. The dog was just as he'd imagined: fairly large, quite hairy, mainly black and white but with brown bits mixed in. Bouncy, friendly, deep amber eyes – the dog of his dreams, jumping up at him, desperate to say hello.

"Rusty, Rusty! Get *down*! I'm so sorry!" Caroline's mum shouted, running towards them. "*Rusty*! What on earth has got into you?"

"Don't worry, I don't mind, I think he's great."

"The feeling seems to be mutual. He's not usually this friendly towards strangers. It's lucky your pony doesn't mind dogs. I'm Caroline's mum, Tracey, by the way. Are you Joe? Caroline's friend from Newbridge Farm?"

Joe nodded. He liked being thought of as Caroline's friend. "Chris is just riding Lady, our other pony, in the indoor school. He wanted me to take Lightning away for a while." Joe said.

Tracey stroked Lightning. "So you're Lightning – the one with navicular—" Her attention switched to the child, who'd started bawling. He'd fallen over by some rose bushes.

Rusty sat down next to Joe, leaning against his leg. Joe held Lightning's lead rope in one hand and fondled the dog's ears. Two amber eyes looked up at him adoringly.

The child carried on crying.

"I'm afraid I'm going to have to take Angus back into the house. He's got a thorn in his hand. If you want to take Lightning for a walk while you're waiting for Chris to finish, just go round the block, as we call it: up there, turn right at the end, follow the fencing alongside the paddocks, carry on past the grain silos, turn right and you'll be back at the house again."

"Okay, thanks," Joe replied.

"Come on Rusty. Here, Rusty!"

Rusty stood, but stayed with Joe, wagging his tail uncertainly.

"Rusty! You really are the most disobedient dog! Come here!"

"Shall I take him with me?" Joe asked hopefully.

"Oh, could you? It would be a huge help. I was just about to give him a walk but I really ought to see to Angus's hand. Just let him in through the back door there when you've finished."

"That's fine. Come on, Rusty," Joe said, not quite believing his luck.

They took the route Tracey had suggested. It felt completely right to be going for a walk with a pony on one side and a dog on the other.

Balance and harmony ... Yes, there's much more to aikido than I ever realised, Joe thought happily as he stopped to look at a mare and foal in the paddock. In fact, there's much more to life than I ever realised.

Chapter 16

When Joe returned to the indoor school, he was amazed to see Emily sitting on Treacle while Caroline led her around the arena.

"Look at me, Joe! Treacle's the best pony in the world!" Emily said. He hadn't seen her look so happy for weeks.

Joe smiled back, surprised at how pleased he was to have his pony-mad sister back again.

Lady wuffled through her nostrils at Lightning, but she seemed to be much calmer. Chris dismounted. "If we can find you a crash hat, Joe, you can have a go," he said. "She's a nice ride. She's just got rather a bad case of stableitis, that's all."

"Stable-what?" Joe asked. Not another weird horse disease.

"Stableitis. I think horse psychiatrists call it 'separation anxiety'. Basically, it means she latches onto other horses for security. We call it stableitis because it often happens when horses spend a lot of time together in a stable or field."

"Oh. What causes it?" Joe asked.

"Anything which harms their self-confidence, from a traumatic experience at weaning to a fright while out riding. That's the trouble with buying horses – it's hard to tell what's happened to them in the past. You often have to find out the hard way."

"How d'you cure it?"

"Time and patience. Basically, you've got to make Lady put her trust in you rather than Lightning. Easier said than done, I know, but it is possible. She's made huge progress this afternoon, so it shouldn't be too difficult. She really wants to please. Here, bring Lightning to me, and try my riding hat on."

It was a remarkably good fit.

"I haven't ridden for over two years," Joe said.

"Time you started again, then. I'll give you a leg-up. One, two, three . . ."

Joe had never sat on a pony like Lady. Everything

was big: big ears, thick neck, lots of mane, chunky shoulders, wide body and, when he turned to look, a broad, round bottom. How had Chris managed to look so at home on her? He gathered up the reins, remembering instantly how to hold them. It was funny how much was coming back to him without even having to think about it.

"You'll find she's surprisingly responsive, as long as she's relaxed like she is now. Be as soft as possible. Don't use any more pressure than you have to," Chris said.

Keep the surface of the water calm, Joe thought, remembering what Nellie had said. He tried his best to follow Chris's instructions, and was amazed by how obedient Lady was compared to the riding school ponies he remembered. She was much more comfortable than he'd expected, as well, like a huge rocking horse.

"That's fantastic," Chris said as Joe stopped Lady in the centre of the arena. "Please don't take this the wrong way, but you're a better rider than I thought you'd be, which is great because I want to suggest something."

Joe wondered what he was going to say.

"I think that both your ponies could come right if you're willing to put in the work. Would you be prepared to do that?"

"I'll give it a go," Joe replied, "but school starts next week, so I won't have much time." He wondered what on earth he was agreeing to.

"Good. For the next couple of weeks, I'd like you to ride Lady around your fields every day, leading Lighting from her. That way you'll be getting used to riding again and Lady will be learning to trust you. What's more, Lightning will be getting the gentle exercise she needs to make her hooves function properly. After two weeks we'll see how they're both going, and take it from there. It won't take long – an hour out of every day at the most. Okay?"

"Not really," Joe said. "You see, I've never led a pony from another one in my life."

"That's why I'm going to teach you now," Chris said, smiling up at him. "And afterwards we can all ride back down to Newbridge Farm together. I need to exercise Buttons."

Chapter 17

Buttons turned out to be a dark brown thoroughbred mare called Chocolate Buttons – the same horse Joe had seen Chris riding on the day they'd arrived at Newbridge Farm. It seemed more like five months ago than five weeks.

Chris said he'd take the two ponies down the road, just in case Lady met a tractor she didn't like. Emily could ride Treacle, led by Caroline, and Joe could ride Chocolate Buttons. Then afterwards Chris and Caroline would carry on with Treacle and Buttons

"What? You want me to get on a *racehorse?*" Joe

asked. Chris had to be joking.

"Buttons is as sane and sensible as they come. She'll look after you."

"I've taken her out lots of times. She's lovely," Caroline added.

Chocolate Buttons stood quietly by the mounting block in the stableyard. Joe could see the outline of her muscles under her gleaming coat, like a drawing in a biology textbook. He'd dreamed of riding a horse like this, and now, out of the blue, he'd been offered the chance.

His heart thumping, he climbed the mounting block, put his left foot in the stirrup iron and swung himself into the saddle while Chris held Buttons from the other side. Wow! A long, lean neck and neat mane stretched out in front of him, and in the distance two elegant ears seemed to be stuck permanently in the forward position. Joe didn't dare look down; it was best not to know how far away the ground had become. When Buttons moved off, her strides were so smooth that Joe barely registered them. He felt on top of the world as they rode past the house.

The front door opened, and Tracey rushed out with Rusty bounding ahead. Joe's heart flipped at the sight of him.

"Can you take him with you? He's been going crazy in the house, and that chap from the Search and

Rescue Centre's coming to see him this evening. Hopefully he'll be less bouncy if he's had a good walk."

I've got to say something, Joe thought, but what? "I'll take him." There, he'd done it.

"Could you? That'd be great. Make sure he's back by eight, though."

No! That isn't what I meant, he thought desperately, but they were all moving off down the road now, and Buttons was getting alarmingly fidgety.

"Bring Buttons to the front!" Chris called. "She's a racehorse – hates being stuck at the back!"

Joe rode past the ponies, and Buttons instantly became much calmer, striding out purposefully in front of the others, her whole body swinging in supple waves. Joe soon became too far ahead to have a conversation with anyone.

When they reached the driveway, Nellie was there. "Look at you!" she said. "Next stop the Grand National!"

Joe grinned, glad she'd seen him but eager to dismount while everything was still okay. "Can you hold her while I get off? We're changing over here," he said. Once he was on solid ground he'd ask Chris about Rusty. He had to. It'd be his last chance.

However, as soon as the other riders came round the corner they all started talking to Nellie. Emily wanted to tell her how wonderful Treacle was, Chris swapped ideas about Lightning and Lady with her and, before Joe knew what had happened, Chris was on Buttons, Caroline was on Treacle and they were riding down the road with Rusty padding along behind.

With a heavy heart, Joe helped Nellie put the ponies out in the field. Emily was bolder now, but still didn't want to handle Lightning by herself.

"I thought you were pony-mad again," Joe said.

"I love Treacle, but Lightning's too big and scary," Emily said.

"Yes, Treacle's much more your size," Nellie agreed. "But Lightning will do you nicely, Joe. She'll be a fantastic ride once her feet are sorted."

"Well, as long as Mum doesn't make me ride her, that's fine," Emily replied.

Joe's relief that Emily had no intention of taking over Lightning again was overshadowed by his sadness at letting Rusty go. As soon as he could, he went to his room. He couldn't think straight. How could he have let this happen? Rusty was perfect! Why hadn't he said anything? He'd been pathetic, spineless. He didn't deserve to have a dog. What had Sensei Radford said? Respect, courage, honour, good manners, focus and concentration are important all the time. Well, he'd lacked courage, for a start. Joe thought of the horseshoe under his bed, and his wish for a dog rolled up neatly in a nail hole. Fine help that had been – although he had to admit he'd been given several chances. Perhaps it had been doing its best but he hadn't wanted Rusty enough. Why, then, did he feel as if he'd never wanted anything so much in all his life? He looked at his watch. It was twenty minutes past six. What had he got to lose? Courage . . .

He took his mobile phone, ran downstairs, out of the back door, onto the road and up towards Orchard View. As soon as his phone registered a signal, he rang Chris's number. Please let him have his phone on him! Please!

"Hello?" He heard Chris's voice, and the sound of hooves on tarmac in the background. Courage.

"Chris? It's Joe."

"Hi, Joe. Everything okay?"

"Not really, I mean sort of. You know Rusty needs a new home?"

"Yes." The clatter of hooves was louder and more frequent now, and he could hear a horse blowing through its nose. They must be trotting.

"Well, I'd like to give Rusty a home. I'd like to have him, if it isn't too late. I've wanted a dog for ages, and my parents said I could have one so I'm sure it'll be okay. I really do like him a lot. I'd give him a good home, I promise."

Joe could hear Chris laughing. He knew this would happen. He'd be laughed at, told he was a townie, too inexperienced, not the right sort of person to have a dog. The sound of hoof-beats was almost deafening now, like a cavalry charge. Joe could hear Caroline laughing too.

"Behind you!" Chris shouted down the phone.

Joe looked behind to see Chris and Caroline trotting up the road towards him, with Rusty bounding in front.

"What a piece of luck," Chris said, halting Buttons. "Down, Rusty!"

Joe hugged Rusty. "Don't worry, I don't mind."

"Mum's just phoned to say the man from Search and Rescue isn't coming after all because he's decided to take on a puppy instead. We were saying at lunch today how Rusty would be an ideal dog for a boy, and Richard said it was a pity you weren't looking for one. I nearly said something this afternoon."

"I nearly said something too," said Caroline.

"It looks as if Rusty's saying something loud and clear, anyway," Chris said, smiling at the dog as he pressed against Joe, trying to get as close as possible. "We'll bring his basket and some dog food down after we've seen to the horses, if you like."

"Great," Joe said. Was he imagining things? This was the moment he'd been waiting for, longing for.

Now it was happening, it was almost too easy. The riders carried on up the hill. He held on to Rusty's collar, but he made no attempt to follow them.

Joe turned for home with his dog by his side. Yes, he realised, it finally feels like home.

Just before the entrance to Newbridge Farm they met Nellie, out for a walk with Mittens. Joe checked Rusty, expecting him to go for the cat, but he just sniffed at her, tail wagging, wanting to be friends. Mittens purred and wound herself in and out of his legs.

"That's amazing," Joe said. "I thought dogs and cats always hated each other."

Nellie looked amused. "Only if they're given a reason to hate." She stroked Rusty. "Wish come true?"

"Yes." Joe couldn't stop grinning. "It nearly didn't, though. The horseshoe was trying its best, but I wasn't helping much. I didn't realise until it was almost too late."

"Ah, that's the thing about wishes: the more help they get the better they turn out. You'll find some take longer than others, some work in unexpected ways and some carry on forever, with luck. Funny things, wishes. Goodnight."

"Bye, Nellie. See you tomorrow," Joe replied. Then he hurried home, his dog by his side.

Chapter 18

Joe's parents weren't nearly as pleased as he'd hoped they'd be when he returned, bursting with excitement, to introduce Rusty to his new family.

"Honestly, Joe, this really isn't a good time to spring something like this on us," Dad said.

"But you *said* I could have a dog as soon as we could find one, and I've found one!" Joe exclaimed.

"Yes, but I didn't mean immediately! These things take a lot of planning."

"Where's he going to sleep?" Mum asked.

"He's got a basket. Chris and Caroline are bringing

it down. He can sleep in the kitchen," Joe replied.

"No, I'm not having dog hairs and mud in my kitchen, thank you very much."

"I'll take the dog back. I'll say you didn't realise how difficult it would be, with Mum still being poorly. I'm sure they'll understand," Dad said firmly.

"No!"

They all looked at Emily.

"No!" she repeated, hugging Rusty. "You *promised* Joe he could have a dog, and Rusty's lovely. He's the best dog in the whole world!" She scrunched up her nose and giggled as he tried to lick her face. "Why can't he sleep in the spare stable down in the yard? All the big dogs at Caroline's farm sleep outside in kennels."

Joe felt something amazingly like love for his sister.

Their parents looked at each other.

Mum sighed. "Okay, we'll try that and see if it works. But if he keeps us awake by barking all night, or turns out to be a nuisance in any way, he'll have to go. I envisaged having something small – a terrier, for instance. I really can't cope with a great big hairy dog in the house, especially not at the moment. Understood?"

Joe and Emily understood, but Rusty didn't. Day by day, he edged his way into the kitchen until they all forgot he wasn't supposed to be there. Rusty became the family pet, but he was definitely Joe's dog. As soon as he arrived back from school Rusty would latch on to him, following him wherever he went.

The ponies quickly got used to having a dog around the place. Lady seemed to be especially keen on Rusty – so much so that she became brave enough to ride without the company of another horse if he was there too, padding alongside.

Although Joe rode Lady by herself sometimes because it was good for her, most days he took the two ponies out together. He was determined to do everything possible to get Lightning sound. She was now officially his pony, and more than anything he wanted to be able to ride her.

To begin with he found leading off Lady pretty daunting. It was bad enough trying to remember how to control one pony, let alone two, and he got into some terrible muddles. Sometimes the reins became mixed up with the lead rope, or Lightning got too far in front, tipping him forwards, or too far behind, nearly pulling him off backwards. But every day he became more confident.

He'd never taken much notice of the seasons before. The autumn and spring terms had meant football and summer had meant athletics, cricket and then a long holiday. Now, however, with ponies and a dog to exercise, he was acutely aware of the changing daylight and weather as summer gradually turned into autumn. Rain or shine, though, he stuck to his routine of exercising the ponies after school.

Sometimes Chris or Caroline, or both of them, came by and they all went out for a ride. Joe loved it when that happened because they went to new places and Chris led Lightning for him so he could concentrate on riding Lady properly. She still didn't like tractors much, but she was getting bolder.

Every Sunday, Joe took the ponies up to the indoor school at Lucketts Farm for a riding lesson on Lady with either Chris or Tracey. Rusty always tagged along, totally at home in both places – so much so that Joe wondered whether he realised he'd officially moved. Now the lucky dog had the best of both worlds.

Occasionally Chris lunged Lightning in circles to see how she was progressing, and every time he said how much she'd improved.

Lady was also improving in her own way. Not only did she seem happier and more confident, but she also showed genuine affection towards Joe and other people she knew.

These mini-triumphs gave Joe the will to carry on,

no matter what the weather was doing or how much homework he had. The only day off he gave himself was Saturday, when he went into Bellsham with Martin and Caroline for an aikido lesson and some fun in town afterwards with Darren, Jake and several other friends.

"You've done a great job here, Joe," Mum said one evening as they were feeding the ponies.

"Well, it's given me something to do," Joe said, stroking Lightning to hide how awkward he felt at being praised.

"No, I mean it. You turned everything around, and I want you to know how grateful I am."

"Wasn't only me. Nellie, Chris and the Coxes helped too."

"I know, but you're the one who's put in the hard work. You didn't have to, but you stuck with it, and turned what could have been a disaster into a blessing. The ponies, and Rusty, have brought us all together in a way I'd never imagined. There, I've said it. I'll go back to being the moody, unreasonable mother you know and love now."

"Phew! Thank goodness for that!" Joe said.

Mum was well again, so at least that wish, *Get well Mum*, had come true. *My own dog* had worked out too.

What were the other ones? He could barely remember ... *England team*, of course, but that was a long shot and he'd never expected it to come true. He didn't have much time for football now, anyway. *Go home.* He'd meant Birmingham when he'd written that, but now Newbridge Farm was home, so that was okay. *Friends.* Yes, he had plenty of friends. *Fortune.* Well, Nellie did say some wishes took longer than others! That made six. What was the seventh? Ah, yes! *Good energy.* That could mean anything, couldn't it? But he had to admit that it felt as if there was a lot of good energy around the place. It was odd none of his wishes had involved horses, although his life seemed to revolve around them now ...

"I've been thinking," Mum said. "You know Dad always jokes we've become a horse rehabilitation centre, what with Lady's insecurities and Lightning's foot problems? Well, there must be so many horses and ponies out there who'd come right with a little bit of care. Wouldn't it be great if we could give them a second chance? We've got the space, I've got the time to look after them and Nellie's keen to help too. What do you think?"

Joe smiled. "Great. I'm up for it if you are."

"I think I'm allergic to form-filling," Mum said,

putting on her glasses and sitting down at the table with a form for opening a new bank account.

"You should be used to it, having been a teacher for so many years," Dad commented.

"That's probably what put me off for life." Mum sat, her pen poised above the paper. "See? I've fallen at the first fence. It's asking for the name of the business, and I haven't even thought of that yet."

"It's obvious – Newbridge Farm, of course," Dad said.

"Mm, The Newbridge Farm Horse and Pony Rehabilitation Centre? It's a bit of a mouthful, isn't it? We need something horsey in the title so the words 'Horse and Pony' aren't needed. And perhaps 'Sanctuary' is a better word. I thought about The Lucky Horseshoe Sanctuary, but that could be confusing, with Lucketts Farm just up the road."

"I know! The Happy Horseshoe Sanctuary!" Emily shouted, jumping up from her chair, astonished by her own brilliance.

"Ugh, too twee," Joe said.

Emily stuck out her tongue at him. "You do better, then, smarty-pants!"

"Okay, how about The Hidden Horseshoe Sanctuary?" Joe said.

Emily pouted and sat down again.

"You know, that's not bad," Dad remarked. "Not

bad at all. I mean, we're certainly off the beaten track here, aren't we?"

"Yes, and it's even more appropriate after what I found today," Mum said, looking at Joe. "A horseshoe!"

Joe felt his cheeks burning with embarrassment. She'd discovered his horseshoe! He should have hidden it better. How silly to put it in that box under the bed, where anyone could find it.

"It must be Lady's shoe," Mum went on. "You know, the one she lost just after she arrived. It was by the trees in the far corner of the field. I thought it would be a nice idea to hang it above our front door for good luck, or kushti bok, as Nellie would say."

"Excellent idea," Dad replied. "From my limited experience of horses and ponies, I think the Hidden Horseshoe Sanctuary will need all the luck it can get!"

Mum made a face at him, and carried on filling in the form.

Joe smiled to himself. With luck he'd be riding Lightning soon ... With luck she'd become sound enough to race again ... With luck, anything seemed possible.

Joe and the Lightning Pony,

the second book in the trilogy,
is available from July 2013.

Here is a preview of the first chapter.

Chapter 1

Joe zipped up his jacket, checked there were gloves among the pony nuts and chaff in its pockets, took his riding hat off the shelf, opened the back door and hesitated.

Rusty bounded into the sleety rain with a joyous bark.

The countryside looked cold, grey and uninviting. It was difficult to remember how green Newbridge Farm had been when they'd moved in last summer – impossible to imagine the sun-baked fields now, in the muddy depths of winter.

I'm sure it never rained this much in Birmingham, Joe thought. Perhaps I just didn't notice, being indoors most of the time. He pulled the hood of his jacket over his head and made a dash for the old farmyard, wincing when ice-cold drops splashed against his face.

Three horses whinnied from their stables.

As Joe approached, Lady pawed at her door impatiently.

"Stop that, you hooligan." He paused to rub her broad forehead, and she bulldozed into his jacket with her hairy muzzle, seeking out the pony nuts in his pocket. She didn't look like a "Lady" at all, with her thick-set body and haphazard black-and-white markings. Her shaggy winter coat, which attracted mud like a magnet, did nothing to enhance her appearance either. Even so, she'd always have a special place in his heart because it was she who'd got him riding again. And Lady didn't realise it, of course, but if Joe hadn't persuaded his parents to give her a second chance, she and Lightning could have had a very different future – or no future at all.

He moved on to Lightning. She bent her elegant head to greet him, her nostrils flickering gently. He still couldn't really get his head round the fact that he had a pony, let alone this one. Everything about her was pretty well perfect, except for her feet. Perhaps even they were a good thing, though, because if she hadn't appeared to be incurably lame her previous owner wouldn't have given her away for free as a companion for Lady ...

Lightning was the reason why Joe didn't mind

getting up on a bleak Sunday morning in mid-December. Chris and Caroline had arranged to meet him so they could go for a ride together. Chris was a farrier, and it was he who'd suggested trying to cure Lightning's lameness by taking her shoes off and giving her the right balance of food and exercise. Touch wood, it seemed to be working.

Caroline, Chris's stepsister, was in the same form as Joe at school. Could she be another reason why he didn't mind getting up early to go for a ride? If so, he definitely wouldn't admit it to anyone, least of all himself.

Lady banged at her stable door again.

"Okay, okay. Hang on a minute," Joe said, moving on to the next horse, always careful not to let any of them feel left out.

Ethel's Tune, a big bay thoroughbred, was the first official resident of The Hidden Horseshoe Sanctuary – Mum's new venture at Newbridge Farm. The idea was to provide a relaxing rehabilitation centre where horses with problems could be treated and, if possible, go on to lead useful lives.

"Morning, ET. Sleep well?" Joe asked, knowing full well what the answer would be if she could talk. As usual, she'd worn a path in the bedding around the edge of her stable where she'd walked round and round all night long. "You'll never get better and win races again if you don't rest your legs, you know," he said, stroking her rigid neck.

The owner of a high-maintenance horse like ET wasn't likely to keep her if she couldn't race or do anything useful. Horses cost a huge amount to look after, and most owners wanted something back in return. At least ET had been given the chance to come right. Joe couldn't bear to think of what might happen to her if she didn't. "You don't realise how important it is, do you?" he said, picking a piece of straw out of her forelock.

She nudged Joe, then her attention switched to some distant point. She stood with her head erect, whinnied, withdrew into her stable and paced around again.

Joe went into the tack room and mixed up three feeds: pony nuts, alfalfa mix and supplements for Lady and ET and a couple of handfuls of pony nuts for Lightning. She'd get a good meal when they returned from their ride. One of the many things Chris had taught him was that horses shouldn't have a lot to eat just before they were ridden.

ET pinned her ears back and looked positively evil as Joe approached with her breakfast. He'd found she backed off when he entered her stable, but he still didn't trust her completely. He edged past, tipped her feed into the manger, ducked underneath her neck and left as quickly as he could. She ate frantically, pawing at the air with alternate forefeet, as if miming a shovelling action.

I'd love to know what's made her such a bundle of nerves, Joe thought. The point-to-pointers at Lucketts Farm are much more laid back, so thoroughbreds aren't all crazy – not if they're treated right.

He hurried on to give Lady her feed. She thrust her head into the bucket as Joe walked into her stable, nearly knocking it out of his hand. "Get over, you greedy pig," he muttered, pushing against her so he could squeeze between the wall and the solid bulk of her body. It's lucky horses are vegetarians, he thought. If Lady were a carnivore she'd be terrifying.

Lightning waited politely, and ate her nuts with unhurried enjoyment while Joe groomed her. Even though she wasn't clipped, she had such fine hair that Joe had bought her a turnout rug to wear in the field during the day and a stable rug to wear at night. The rugs kept her clean as well as warm, which was ideal because grooming horses caked in mud wasn't his idea of fun.

He'd nearly finished tacking up Lightning when there was a clatter of hooves in the yard. "Good timing!" he called. Glancing over the stable door, he noticed that Chris was riding Chocolate Buttons and Caroline was on another thoroughbred horse.

"Where's Treacle?" he asked.

"I've got him here," Chris said. "We thought Emily might like to come too. I can lead her off Buttons."

Joe took a proper look and saw Treacle, Caroline's little Dartmoor pony, standing happily between the two thoroughbreds, his large, inquisitive eyes peering through his dripping forelock.

"I think Emily's having a lie-in," Joe said. She wouldn't want Chris and Caroline to know that, but it irritated him that she always told everyone how much she loved horses when she rarely helped look after them.

"Oh. Can you go and see?" Chris asked.

"Okay." Joe hitched Lightning's rein underneath her stirrup for safety, and trudged back to the house. He'd been getting on better with his younger sister since they'd moved to Newbridge Farm but, even so, he enjoyed spending time alone with the horses and riding with Caroline and Chris. He'd turned out to be the one who really liked horses and was keen enough to do the hard work as well as enjoy the fun. Horses had become his thing, and he wanted it to stay that way.

Author`s Notes

I loved horse and pony stories when I was a girl, and I've kept my favourite books from childhood: *Black Beauty*, *Silver Snaffles*, *My Friend Flicka*, *Cobbler's Dream*, *Misty of Chincoteague*, *The Black Stallion*, *Moorland Mousie*, *Fly-by-Night*, *The Team*, *Flambards* ... The full list would go on for pages. These stories often had a boy as a main character, or at least a major one, and were more enjoyable for it – like a party where everyone's invited.

However, although boys still ride and men take part in all sorts of top-level equestrian sports, girls seem to monopolise modern horse and pony stories. In many parts of the world a pony culture exclusively for girls has grown up, awash with pinks and purples. It takes a brave boy to carry on riding regardless, but a surprising number do, and that's why I wanted to write this story. It's the first in a trilogy about Joe's ponies and horses, and whether you're a boy or girl, man or woman, I hope you enjoy it.

I would like to thank my husband, Chris, for his support, his illustrations and for the horses he's shared with me over the years. He longed for a pony when he was growing up on his parents' farm in North Devon, but he didn't have a horse of his own until he was an adult and could buy one for himself. His parents borrowed a pony for him one summer, but his excitement soon turned to bitter disappointment because, like Lady in this story, the pony wouldn't be caught. When Chris did eventually catch and ride it, he was bucked off. Unlike Joe, he wasn't lucky enough to have knowledgeable neighbours who were willing to lend a hand, so the pony enjoyed a holiday for the rest of the summer.

Since we've been married, Chris and I have had several horses and ponies, each with particular strengths and weaknesses. Needless to say, we discovered most of their weaknesses after we'd bought them. We've never been able to afford expensive ones, so we've usually ended up with horses with mental or physical problems, or both! A common difficulty has been "stableitis", or a fear of being separated from equine companions. So when I was thinking of a problem Lady might have, that seemed like an obvious choice.

Lightning's problem, navicular syndrome, was chosen because it's a problem which, until recently, was thought to be largely incurable, but recent research has shown horses with it often benefit from going "barefoot" together with appropriate food and exercise. Navicular syndrome is especially common in horses and ponies that do a lot of fast work and turning, but you'll find out more about Lightning's past in the sequel to this story, *Joe and The Lightning Pony*.

There's a clue to Lightning's past in Joe's discovery that she takes off when she hears words sounding like *go*. Several years ago we owned a Clydesdale cart horse called Blue. He'd been taught to obey voice commands, and if you said any word that sounded remotely like *whoa* (*Joe*, *go*, *no* or *low*, for instance) he'd screech to a halt, no matter how fast he was travelling. We chose our words very carefully after a while!

For a long time I have been fascinated by Romany

culture, and for several years I was lucky enough to own a Romany vardo. The idea for the wishing shoe came from a friend with strong Romany connections.

Mark Rashid is an American horse trainer who has written some excellent books about his experiences helping all sorts of horses and horse owners. He also teaches aikido, and applies many of the principles of aikido to horsemanship. His ideas on the subject really struck a chord with me when I read them, and I have found them useful when handling our own horses, especially our free-living Exmoor ponies. Andrew Medland, instructor at aikido shudokan, kindly allowed me to observe some of his lessons and lent me several books about aikido, for which I am very grateful.

Tom and Victoria, friends who live nearby, shared some of their experiences of moving to the countryside. For instance, there were some silage bales ...

There is a strong theme of farriery throughout this trilogy. Our farrier, Clive Ley, and his assistants, Josh and Dusty, put up with me watching them at work, taking photos and asking endless questions about horseshoes and shoeing. Their input was really useful, and chocolate biscuits are now assured when they come to our farm to shoe our horses!

I'm also very grateful to Nic Barker, our local

"barefoot farrier" for sharing so much information with me about horse hoof rehabilitation and keeping horses unshod. She suggested a scenario for Lightning's recovery from apparently incurable lameness, based on her experiences with many similar cases.

Finally, many thanks to Fiona Kennedy and Felicity Johnston, my editors at Orion Children's Books, for giving me a perfect combination of freedom, guidance and encouragement.

Sign up for **the orion star**
newsletter to get inside information
about your favourite children's authors
as well as exclusive competitions and
early reading copy giveaways.

www.orionbooks.co.uk/newsletters

Follow on